Indulge With Me

a with me in seattle celebration

Indulge
with me

a with me in seattle celebration

Short Stories by *New York Times* Bestselling Author
KRISTEN PROBY

Recipes from *USA Today* Bestselling Author
SUZANNE M. JOHNSON

EVIL EYE
CONCEPTS

Indulge With Me

ISBN: 978-1-948050-65-4

Published by Evil Eye Concepts, Incorporated

Introduction

I've always thought that food and love speak the same language. When my husband wants to surprise me, he knows I'd much rather receive a pie than a vase full of flowers. Roses are beautiful, but how can they hold a candle to huckleberries? Afterwards, we get to share the bounty while we catch up on our days.

Coming home to my *With Me In Seattle* series after spending so much time away, I couldn't think of a better way to catch up with the Montgomerys than over a meal. It inspired a lot of daydreaming about my old friends—which is truly how I see the characters I've lived with for so long. What do their lives look like now? What are they celebrating after their happy endings? If I came over, what would they serve me? One thing was certain. Comfort food and laughter in a cozy kitchen is the perfect way to reconnect.

Luckily for me, my friend and chef Suzanne Johnson shares my vision of family, friends, and food. Through her wonderful recipes and the brand-new stories I wrote to accompany them, six of my favorite love stories have come back to life, on the page and in the kitchen. In some ways, I've gotten to know Suzanne as well as I know Luke and Natalie. I guess you could say she's an honorary Montgomery at this point!

From the bottom of my heart, thank you for joining Suzanne and me as Seattle comes back to delicious, loving life—this time, with *you*.

Love,

Kristen

Table of Contents

CHAPTER 1: BRUNCH

Brunch Recipes

CHAPTER 2: GAME DAY

Game Day Recipes

CHAPTER 3: A ROCKSTAR REUNION

A Rockstar Reunion Recipes

CHAPTER 4: DINNER PARTY

Dinner Party Recipes

CHAPTER 5: HOUSEWARMING PARTY

Housewarming Party Recipes

CHAPTER 6: GIRLS NIGHT- COCKTAILS & SHENANIGANS

Cocktails & Shenanigans Recipes

Jules and Nate

cordially invite you to

a brunch

celebrating the engagement of

Wyatt & Amelia

Sunday ~ 10am

on the sand at their beach house

RSVP to Jules by Friday morning

Jules & Nate

Jules

"I'm so excited for you both," I say, my champagne glass lifted in the air, toasting my cousin, Amelia and her fiancé, Wyatt. "Congratulations."

"Congratulations," everyone says happily, toasting the couple glowing with happiness. Lia and Wyatt got engaged a few months ago, and I wanted to host a party for them then, but the summer got away from us and getting our whole family together these days isn't an easy task.

But I was finally able to arrange for everyone, and I mean *everyone,* to come to our beach house to celebrate the engagement. All of our families are here, including Amelia's parents and siblings, Wyatt's parents and two brothers, and all of my crazy brood.

I think there are more than thirty people in our home.

And I freaking love it.

I would normally hire my sister-in-law, Alecia, to organize a party of this size, but I really wanted to do this for Lia, and I'm pleased with the outcome.

"By the way, everyone," I continue after Wyatt dips Lia down for a passionate kiss and everyone applauds, "the food is ready and set up, thanks to McCollum Catering, and it looks absolutely delicious."

"That's where I'm headed," Will, my football player brother, immediately says.

"Me, too," Archer, Lia's brother says, high-fiving Will.

"And," I say, giving both men the stink eye, making them halt in their tracks, "we have an array of cupcakes courtesy of our very own Nic."

"Thank the good Lord," Samantha Nash says, raising her hands in the air and making us all laugh.

"I have a mimosa and bloody Mary station set up down at the gazebo, so feel free to raid that. Have fun, everyone."

The crowd disperses, most of the men headed straight for the food, which makes me grin. Alecia comes walking over with a smug smile on her pretty lips.

"Hey there," I say and wrap her in a hug.

"This party is seriously amazing," she says, and pops something in her mouth. "And these fried glazed donuts? Jesus Christ, I think I just had an orgasm."

I giggle and reach for one of my own, sighing as it practically melts in my mouth. "Girl. Get me away from them. I'll eat them all. I'm so glad you approve. I was nervous about taking it on myself."

"You didn't need me," she says, shaking her head. "This setting is so beautiful, you don't need a lot of fluff. The food is delicious, and speaking of which, how did you find this caterer?"

"Nate and I have an inside joke," I reply with a chuckle and smile when my brother Dominic joins us, wrapping his arm around his wife's waist. "I've called this caterer his *minions* since we were dating. Whenever we came here, he'd call ahead and they would come in and set everything up before we arrived, so it just sort of magically happened. I love them."

"Well, I need to get the minion's info from Nate because I'm planning a beach wedding next summer, and I could use them."

"I thought you weren't planning weddings anymore, now that you're working full time at the winery?" I ask, accepting a mimosa from my husband, Nate, as he joins us. Alecia smiles as he passes one to her as well.

My husband is larger than life, and still sets my skin on fire as soon as he comes in a room. I want to climb him pretty much 24/7, and I pray that never goes away.

"This one is for a friend," Alecia says with a small shrug. "I couldn't tell her no when she asked for my help."

"My *tesoro* spreads herself too thin," Dom says, kissing Alecia's temple. His voice is still thick with an Italian accent, despite living in the States for many years.

"I'm fine," Alecia insists. "And this is a hell of a party. And speaking of parties, don't forget we're hosting one at the vineyard in a couple of weeks."

"I wouldn't forget it," I promise and reach out to pat my brother on the shoulder. "We're so proud of you, Dom."

His lips curl up into a smile, and he leads Alecia away. I take a sip of my drink, surveying the scene.

"Everyone's fine," Nate whispers into my ear, tugging me against his side. "And you're fucking beautiful in this dress."

I glance down at the silver shift dress, cinched at the waist with a Gucci belt, and grin up at him. "It's the heels, isn't it?"

I mean, the brand new black Louboutins got him hard when I took them out of the box yesterday. He's barely taken his eyes off of them.

"I'm going to fuck you in nothing but those shoes," he promises, and everything in me catches on fire. He's not lying. My ankles will be wrapped around his neck later tonight, and I'll be wearing these shoes.

I can't fucking wait.

"Getting me all hot and bothered when we have dozens of guests isn't nice."

His face transforms into that sexy smile that says *I don't give a fuck.*

"I never claimed to be nice, Julianne. Be sure to eat some food."

And with that, he kisses my cheek and walks away to talk to my brother Caleb.

I take a deep breath, and then a long drink of my mimosa. I could use another, although I rarely drink when my daughter, Stella, is around.

I search the crowd for her and smile when I see that she's on my best friend Natalie's lap, eating a chocolate cinnamon roll. I cringe inside, hoping no one lets her overdose on sugar today. I don't need her to be high on sweets all day.

But then I shrug. Today is a day for celebration. She can have some sugar.

"Jules." Amelia rushes over to me, panting, her eyes wide in horror. "I have an emergency."

"Did you start your period?" I ask, whispering loudly. "Shit, you're wearing white. Do you need a pad?"

"No, Jesus, I didn't start my period. It's much worse."

"Worse than your period in a white dress?"

She nods and swallows hard, trying to catch her breath. "I lost my ring."

I stare at her for a moment, trying to register the words coming out of her mouth, then glance down at her naked left hand.

"Wait. Your *engagement* ring?"

"Shh!" She covers her mouth with her fingers and leans in closer. "Yes, my engagement ring, and Wyatt *can't* know."

"Where the hell did you lose it?"

"In the bathroom."

I take her elbow and pull her to the guest bathroom, just as Nic approaches it as well.

"Sorry, I'll find a different bathroom," she says, then stops and narrows her eyes at us. "What's going on?"

"Lia lost her engagement ring," I reply and hurry into the restroom, flipping on the light as I go.

"Never mind, I'm staying right here," Nic says, following. "How did you lose it?"

"I don't know! I came in to use the restroom, and I washed my hands. I always take it off when I wash them because I don't want it to get full of soap residue."

"First mistake," I mutter. "Just take it in to get cleaned once a month. Trust me on this one."

"Well, *now* I know," she says and bites her lip. "Anyway, I set it on the vanity, and I must have forgotten to put it back on. So I left the bathroom, and realized that I didn't have it about ten minutes later, but when I came back, it was *gone*."

Her voice is wavering, and her eyes fill with tears, and my perfect party is about to spontaneously combust.

"It fell down the drain," Nic says simply. "It's easy to fish out. We just need a wrench."

"Do you have a wrench?" Lia asks me with hope-filled eyes.

"Of course I do," I reply with false confidence. I'm not even sure what *kind* of wrench we need, but I'm determined to fix this. "I'll be right back."

I run out to the garage and root around for a couple of wrenches of all sizes, hoping that I get one that will do the trick, and hurry back in to find Lia sitting on the toilet with her head between her knees and Nic rubbing circles on her back.

"I'm gonna pass out," Lia mumbles.

"No, you're not. See? We've got this."

I show them the wrenches, and Nic scowls. "That one is way too small."

"What about these?" I ask, showing her the others I found.

"That big one might work."

I discard the others, open the cabinet to the pipes, and all three of us struggle to get on the floor.

"I'm wearing *way* too tight of a dress for this," Nic says with a scowl. "Seriously, someone's going to walk in here and see up my skirt to my vagina and Matt's gonna be *pissed*. He'll spank me."

"Why aren't you wearing panties?" Lia asks.

"Because Matt forbade it," Nic replies as if she just said that her hair is brown.

"Excuse me," Lia says, stopping me from trying to fit the wrench on the pipe. "Did you just say he *forbade it*?"

Nic grins. "Oh yeah. And it's sexy as fuck when he gets all dominant on me. It's our thing."

"Huh. I had no idea," Lia says.

"But now you're going to get me in trouble," Nic says, sticking her lower lip out.

"Oh, for Godsake. Pull it together." I roll my eyes and kick my brand new shoes off in frustration. "Take one for the team here, Nic."

"I'm down here, aren't I?" she replies and lays back to take a look at the pipe. "Here, hand me the wrench."

I happily comply, and Lia and I join her, lying under the sink and watching her try to fit the wrench around the silver pipe.

"How is it dusty under here?" I wonder aloud. "Like, how does dust actually get *under* the sink? Isn't that defying the laws of gravity or something?"

"I found dust *inside* my shoes," Lia says with a shrug. "I think the dust is alive."

"That's disgusting."

Nic grunts with the exertion of trying to turn the wrench and then collapses on the ground. "This thing is on there tight."

"Oh my God, you guys, we *have* to find it." Lia shakes her head and wipes under her eyes. "And I need my emergency makeup bag from the car because I refuse to spend my engagement party looking like a goddamn raccoon."

"Oh, honey, you don't look like a raccoon." I pat her shoulder, but she turns wet eyes to me.

"I will if we don't find my ring."

"I'm gonna get this mother fucker off," Nic says, grunting again as she tries to turn the wrench.

"Would it help if I push as you pull?" I ask her and try to get some leverage under the sink to help. "God, it's so uncomfortable down here. How do plumbers do it?"

"They're not in tiny dresses and heels," Nic grumbles, blowing a piece of her hair out of her eyes. "Lia, you owe me a makeover after this."

"I'll come to your house and do your makeup every damn day if you find my ring," Lia pledges, holding up her hand as if she's swearing on the Bible. "I'll carry babies for you."

Nic smiles softly. "Thanks for the offer, but we're adopting."

"*WHAT*?" I shriek and pull her into my arms for a hug. "You are? When? You have to tell me *everything*."

"After we find my ring," Lia says. "And yes, we need all of the details."

Because of PCOS and diabetes, Nic didn't think she'd ever be able to have children. My brother, Matt, has been amazingly supportive and wonderful, but I didn't know they'd decided to adopt. I couldn't be more excited for them.

"Thanks," Nic says with a goofy smile. "She'll be here in just a few months."

"*She*?" I pull her in for another hug. "Another baby girl in our family!"

"Oh no," Lia says, tears streaming down her face. "I'm totally a raccoon now, and I don't care. Nic, I'm so excited for you."

"Matt's so cute about it," Nic says as she props her head in her hand. "He's already bought some little outfits and stuff, but you guys, I haven't bought anything. I don't want to get my hopes up too high."

"Why?" Lia asks.

"What if the birth mom changes her mind?" Nic whispers. "What if something horrible happens with the pregnancy?"

"Oh sweetheart, don't talk like that."

"I know, it's totally horrible to think this way, but I can't help it. I'm terrified that I'll be standing in that birthing room with her, and the baby will come, and the birth mom will tell me that she can't give her to me."

Nic turns worried brown eyes to me. "I get it. I couldn't give my baby up," I reply and pet her arm, trying to reassure her. "But she's doing this for a reason, Nic. Maybe she doesn't have a choice. Or she just knows that she can't provide for the baby like you can, and she's doing the bravest, most wonderful thing in the world. She's so fucking amazing."

"I know," Nic says, swallowing hard. "We got to meet her, and she's really nice. I'm just trying to keep it together until all is said and done and the papers are signed."

Lia pulls her phone out of a pocket I didn't even know she had.

"Shit, guys. Wyatt just texted and wants to know where I am."

"Back to the task at hand," Nic says, pulling on the wrench again. "Damn it, I don't know if I can get this fucker off."

"Why do men screw them on so tight? Are they just trying to prove how strong they are?" I ask.

"Or, you know, trying to prevent leaks," Nic says with a smirk.

"Or that," I agree. "Hold please." I reach up and flip a switch. "There, the floor will heat up. My ass is getting cold."

"Good call," Lia says. "But let's hurry this along. He'll come looking for me any minute."

"Should we try a different screwy thing?" I ask, checking out the pipe. "It looks like it might attach here, too."

"Maybe," Nic says, thinking it over. "I just didn't want to make too much of a mess."

"I don't give a shit about the mess, let's just get the ring out, and then we can clean up."

"Yes, that's the best plan," Lia says, nodding vigorously. "It came in a red box, you guys. This isn't a cheap ring, or easy to replace."

"Okay, pass me the middle wrench," Nic says, holding her hand out, and I pass it to her, feeling like I'm assisting a surgeon.

"I didn't expect to spend today like this," I admit with a laugh. "We'll think it's funny ten years from now."

Suddenly, someone clears their throat from the doorway, and we all stop moving, staring at each other, until my husband says, "What, exactly, are you doing?"

Nate

I haven't seen Julianne in more than ten minutes. It's unlike her to disappear at a party, especially when she's hosting, but every time I try to go search for her, I get sidetracked by another family member.

I never expected when I was growing up with just me and my dad that I'd end up in a family with the population of Arizona. It's everything I never knew I needed.

"Did you have some of this quiche?" Caleb asks as he goes back for seconds.

"Not yet," I reply.

"Well, you'd better hurry because I'm about to decimate it." He laughs and digs in.

I keep going back for the crab cakes. The spread is impressive, and I'll have to send a personal note of thanks to the master chef, Suzanne. She's never let me down.

I wander over to Natalie and smile at my daughter, who's perched on Nat's lap.

"Hi there, peaches."

"Hi, Daddy." She smiles and takes a bite of a donut.

"Have you been eating lots of sugar?"

Her eyes widen and she shakes her head innocently, but Natalie laughs and nods.

"Hmm. No more after that donut, okay?"

Stella grins, sugar coating her tiny pink lips and bats her eyes at me. "Maybe just one more?"

"No."

"Half of one?"

I laugh and lean in to kiss her plump cheek. At almost five years old, she's losing some of her baby fat and changing so quickly. I hate the thought of her growing up.

"You can have *one* more. Aunt Natalie is going to make sure you don't eat more than that."

"I won't," Stella promises and presses her sugary lips to my cheek.

"Have you seen Julianne?" I ask Nat, who frowns and glances around.

"No, not in a little while. I saw her talking with Lia a bit ago. They're probably down getting mimosas or something."

I nod and walk across the wraparound porch to the steps that lead down to the gazebo.

I didn't know it at the time, but buying this beach house was the best decision I could have made in real estate close to ten years ago. I bought it for a low price, and it's only appreciated in value.

More than that, our family loves it and uses it often. It's less than two hours from Seattle, making it the perfect getaway spot.

"Hey, Nate, thanks for hosting this," Wyatt, the groom-to-be, says as I reach the gazebo and drink station. He shakes my hand. "We appreciate it."

"It's no trouble at all," I reply. "Have you seen Jules?"

"No. In fact, I haven't seen Amelia in a bit either. I texted her, but haven't heard back."

I nod. "They're probably together, getting in trouble."

"I think Amelia brought some makeup stuff for a few of the girls, so you're probably right," Wyatt says, physically relaxing.

"You were worried about her."

His eyes meet mine and then he shrugs. "Of course. I love her. It's what I do."

"You're going to fit into this family just fine," I reply, clapping him on the shoulder. "I'll go look for them."

"I'll join you," Wyatt says and follows me back up the stairs.

When we reach the top, Matt is about to descend the stairs, his face tight and lips thin.

"What's wrong?" I ask him.

"I can't find Nic," he replies. "I was going to check down there."

"She's not there," Wyatt says. "We think the girls are checking out makeup stuff that Amelia bought. We're going to look for them."

Matt's shoulders relax and he nods. "Let's go."

We walk into the house, past kids running about and parents sitting and talking, laughing and enjoying the day.

"Back here," I say. "I bet they're in the bathroom."

I lead them to the guest bathroom, silently open the door, and the scene before us has all of us stopping in our tracks.

Three sets of legs, all long and smooth, are sticking out from under the sink. Their matching torsos are inside the cabinet, and the girls are giggling and talking.

I glance at Wyatt and Matt, and both of them just smile and shrug. Wyatt leans his shoulder against the doorframe, Matt crosses his arms over his chest, and I shove my hands in my pockets, then say, "What, exactly, are you doing?"

All activity below the sink comes to a halt as they freeze. Wyatt smirks next to me, and we wait for the girls to decide what to do next.

Julianne is in the middle. Her shoes, the ones that have kept me semi-hard for hours, are discarded on the bathroom floor. Lia is to our left and Nic is to our right.

There are wrenches on the floor.

I can't wait to hear what this is all about.

Jules' head pokes out from under the cabinet and she sends us a sweet smile.

"Hi."

"Hello, my love. What's up?"

"Oh, we're just doing some home improvement work under here."

I cock a brow as Wyatt snickers. Matt shifts, and when I glance at him, he's got a huge smile on his face.

"I didn't realize you were a do-it-yourselfer," I reply and Jules bites her lower lip, making my cock twitch.

I'd like to make her bite that lip for more carnal reasons.

But that will come later.

"I'm usually not," she admits. "Nic's much better than me with a wrench."

"I had no idea," Matt says, and Nic's head comes out from under the sink in surprise. "Hello, little one."

"Hey, babe," she says and offers him a small wave.

"Don't you think your skirt is a bit short to be on the floor?" Matt asks her and she shakes her head.

"No, I'm perfectly fine."

Matt tilts his head, looking up her legs, his arms still crossed.

"Really? Because I can see farther up that skirt than I'm comfortable seeing in mixed company."

"You picked it out," she reminds him.

"I didn't anticipate you crawling under the sink."

"If you're still hiding under there because you think we can't see you, you're wrong, sweetheart," Wyatt says and Amelia lets out a deep sigh before joining the other two, sitting on the bathroom floor.

Her bright blue eyes are full of tears.

"Hey," Wyatt says, immediately concerned, and squats next to her, cupping her cheek. "What's going on?"

"We're trying to take the pipes apart," Lia says with a quivering voice, "because I think I dropped my ring down the drain."

My eyes fly to Jules' and she grimaces. "Why didn't you come get me?"

"We thought we could do it by ourselves," Jules says. "But this pipe is on here *really* tightly."

Matt helps Nic to her feet, kisses her cheek, then whispers in her ear and makes her face turn scarlet red. Then he squats down and checks out his wife's handiwork.

"First of all," he begins, "you're doing this wrong."

Wyatt and I help our girls to their feet, and we all stand back to watch Matt work on the pipe. Amelia is sniffling, leaning against Wyatt.

"I'm so sorry," she whispers.

"Hey, it's okay," he says. "We'll find it."

Jules leans closer to Nic. "What did Matt say to you?"

"Trust me, you don't want to know," Nic replies and gives Jules a smug grin. "But things are going to get interesting later."

"Lucky girl," Jules says, nudging her with her elbow.

I plunge my fingers into the back of Jules' hair, fist it, and press my lips to her ear.

"You have no idea what I have planned for you later." The words are so quiet that no one else could possibly hear them. Julianne takes a surprised, quiet breath, and I'm pleased when her cheeks turn pink.

I'm going to make her ass turn pink later.

"There's no ring in here," Matt announces and Amelia gasps.

"But there has to be," she says. "I set it on the vanity."

"Where else have you been?" I ask her.

She takes a deep breath, dries her eyes, and pulls it together.

Good girl.

"I went to the gazebo for a drink. I could use another one."

"Okay," Wyatt says. "Where else?"

"I grabbed something to eat, I ran out to the car for a second to grab some face cleanser for Meredith, and then I came into the bathroom."

"Is your car unlocked?" I ask. Amelia nods.

"Okay," I say, taking charge of the situation. "Wyatt, take Lia down to the gazebo to look around and get the poor woman a drink. Make it a stiff one."

"On it," he says, leading her out of the room.

"Matt and Nic, go check the car. Julianne and I will go check in with our guests and look around the food tables to see if we can find anything."

"Sounds good," Matt says. "Let's go, little one."

Nic grins and follows her husband to the front door, and I lace my fingers through Julianne's and pull her hand to my lips, pressing a kiss on her knuckles. When the other two couples are gone, and before I lead her out to the rest of the party, I pull her into the bathroom and shut and lock the door.

Her wide blue eyes, the same color as Amelia's, meet mine.

"Put your shoes on," I command her. Her lips tip up into a smile, and she does as I ask, slipping her slender feet into her fuck-me heels.

As soon as she has her balance, I pick her up and brace her against the back of the door, kissing her like my life depends on it.

Because I swear, there are moments that it does.

Nothing is more important to me than the woman in my arms and the tiny girl outside that door.

"You make me fucking crazy," I growl into her ear. "It seems I can't go six hours without wanting to be planted inside you. I love you so much I ache with it."

"Yes," she pants, circling her hips and freeing my long hair, running her fingers through it. "I love you, too. So much."

I smile against her lips, set my cock free, and slip easily inside her, making her groan when my apa slides along the most sensitive parts of her pussy.

"Jesus," she whispers as I fuck her hard, one hand reaching back to grip onto her heel.

"You'll still wear these later," I say, burying my face in her neck and biting her, careful not to leave a mark. "But I need this right now."

"Hell yes," she says and whimpers when her orgasm moves through her. She clenches down on me, and the pressure in my spine and balls is out of this fucking world as I lose control.

Once we catch our breath, I set her on her feet, make sure she has her balance, then tuck myself away. As she rights herself, I pull my hair back, and then, with a smug smile on her gorgeous face, we leave the bathroom.

Jules hurries to the buffet line and quickly searches around the food, lifting spoons and spoon rests, hoping the ring fell on the table top.

I pull the table cloth off the ground and look under it, in case it rolled beneath the food.

Nothing.

Matt and Nic wander out from inside the house, Nic sporting the same grin as my wife, and I assume somewhere outside of my beach house has been christened by these two.

"It's not in the car," Matt says. "We'll head down and see if Wyatt and Lia found anything."

"We'll be right behind you," Julianne says and then sighs and looks up at me with worried eyes. "She's going to be devastated if we don't find it."

"Is everything okay, darling?" Julianne's mom, Gail, asks as she joins us. She reaches over to add some ham biscuits with fig jam to her plate. "I need the recipe for these biscuits. They're so flaky."

"Everything's great, Mom," Julianne replies, pasting on her fake smile. "You know how it is, just making sure everyone is having a great time."

Gail narrows her eyes on her daughter, but doesn't call her out on the lie. She just pats her hand and says, "Let me know if I can help. Everyone's having a lovely time. Don't worry."

She wanders back to her seat, next to Wyatt's mom. The two have been thick as thieves for weeks.

"We'll find it, or replace it," I murmur to Julianne. "Let's go down to the gazebo and see what's what."

She nods and leads me down the stairs. Wyatt is sitting on one of the deep couches with Lia curled up next to him. Her tears are gone, but she looks defeated.

Matt and Nic are pouring themselves bloody Marys. Meredith and Stacy are chatting on the opposite couch, drinking mimosas.

"I take it you didn't find it," Julianne says, her shoulders falling in disappointment.

"No," Lia says. "I'm so pissed."

"I'll file an insurance claim," Wyatt replies. "And I can replace it."

"I know, but it's expensive, and it has an immense amount of sentimental value," Lia replies. "I'm so sorry."

"What happened?" Meredith asks.

"I lost my engagement ring."

"Oh, honey," Stacy says. "I'm so sorry."

Lia shrugs. "You know, it sucks, but I'm not going to let it ruin the rest of this party. Everyone is here to celebrate us, and I refuse to mope about this for one more minute."

She stands and holds her hand out to Wyatt.

"I want a chocolate cinnamon roll."

"Let's get you one then," he says as he stands and follows Lia up the stairs.

"I'm sorry to hear that," Meredith says, looking down at her own wedding band and engagement ring. "I had a scare like that once, and I was positive my heart was going to fall out of my chest."

"I *did* lose my wedding band," Stacy says, shaking her head. "When I was pregnant with Michael, my hands were so swollen I couldn't wear my rings, so I put my engagement ring in the safe, but kept my wedding band out for the rare occasions that I could manage to wrangle it on my finger. I set it on the bedside table, and it disappeared. To this day, I don't know where it is. Isaac bought me a new one, but I wish I had the original."

"It happens," I reply and wrap my arm around Julianne's back. "Things can always be replaced. Do you need anything from upstairs?"

"No thanks," Mer says with a smile. "We're enjoying the ocean breeze and the company."

Jules leads me upstairs, and we find seats next to Natalie, Luke, Will and Meg. Stella has moved to Will's lap, and he keeps stealing her nose.

"You don't have my nose!" she exclaims with a laugh.

"Here, I'll put it back," Will says, and presses his fingers to Stella's face, making her laugh harder.

"Mommy," Olivia says as she runs up to Natalie. "Look at my new pretty!"

She holds her hand up to Natalie's face, and Jules and I freeze before glancing at each other.

"Uh, Olivia, I don't think this is for you."

"I found it in the bathroom! Finders keepers, losers weepers."

Jules squats next to Olivia and kisses her cheek. "Baby doll, that's a pretty ring. But you know what?"

"What?"

"That's Miss Lia's ring. She lost it earlier, and you found it for her. She's going to be so excited."

Olivia's beautiful face scrunches into a frown. "But I like it."

"You have lots of costume jewelry at home," Nat says with a laugh. "Please give Aunt Jules the ring."

Olivia slides it off of her finger and drops it in Jules' outstretched palm. "Okay."

"Thanks, baby doll," Jules says before kissing the little girl again and turning to me with a bright smile. "Thank the baby Jesus! We found it!"

Brunch

Ham Biscuits with Fig Jam

Crab Cakes Benedict

Loaded Potato Waffles

Spinach and Strawberry Salad with Poppy Seed Dressing

Chocolate Cinnamon Rolls Topped with Cream Cheese Icing

Blackberry Bread Pudding

Southwest Quiche

Fried Glazed Donuts

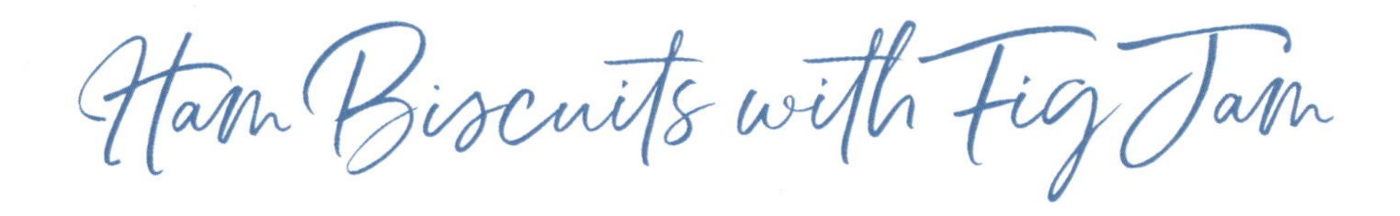

Ham Biscuits with Fig Jam

2 tablespoons butter

1 pound country ham steak

24 Homemade Tea Biscuits

Fig Jam

In a large iron skillet over medium heat, melt butter and add ham steak. Brown on each side for 1-2 minutes. Remove from heat and slice into 1-2 inch pieces. To build the sandwich, slice each biscuit in half and top with 2 slices of ham and ½ to 1 tablespoon of Fig Jam. Serve on a platter with additional jam.

Fig Jam

See page 164

Homemade Tea Biscuits

2 cups self-rising flour

1 teaspoon salt

8 tablespoons (1 stick) butter, chilled and cubed

¾ cup buttermilk

2 tablespoons melted butter

Preheat oven to 425 degrees. Mix together the flour and salt. Cut butter into flour mixture with a fork. Coarse crumbs will appear. Pour in the buttermilk. Stir together to combine. On a lightly floured surface, fold and press dough in a folding pattern 2-3 times, then roll dough until about 1 inch thick. Cut out 24 biscuits using a small biscuit cutter (1½ inch). Place biscuits on a greased cookie sheet and brush the tops with melted butter. Bake for 12-15 minutes or until golden brown.

Crab Cakes Benedict

Crab Cakes

1 pound lump crab meat

4 green onions, chopped

1 egg

½ cup mayonnaise (or Greek yogurt)

1 cup panko breadcrumbs

Juice of one lemon

1 teaspoon minced garlic

1 teaspoon salt

1 teaspoon pepper

8 tablespoons (1 stick) butter

Combine all ingredients except butter and form into 1 inch thick cakes. Melt 2 tablespoons of the butter in a large skillet over medium heat. Place 4 crab cakes in the skillet and cook for 3 minutes on each side or until golden brown. Add more butter as needed to avoid sticking. Remove from skillet and place on paper towels to drain.

Poached Eggs

1 tablespoon white vinegar

8 eggs

The secret to the perfect poached egg is the "vinegar tornado." In a large saucepan, bring 4 cups of water and 1 tablespoon vinegar to a boil. Reduce heat to simmer. Crack an egg in a small bowl. Using a large spoon, begin stirring the boiling water until a tornado forms. Gently drop the egg into the middle of the tornado and cook until the whites are set but the yolk is still runny, about 2 minutes. Remove the egg with a slotted spoon and place on paper towels to drain. Repeat with remaining eggs.

Easy Hollandaise

½ cup mayonnaise

½ teaspoon Dijon mustard

1 tablespoon lemon juice

½ teaspoon cayenne pepper

½ teaspoon salt

2 tablespoons salted butter

Using a blender, mix together mayonnaise, Dijon mustard, lemon juice, cayenne pepper and salt until blended well. Melt butter in a microwave safe dish for 20-30 seconds then add to blender while continuing to blend.

To Build Benedict

Place one crab cake on a dish and top with poached egg and hollandaise. Repeat with remaining eggs and enjoy.

Loaded Potato Waffles

1 package instant mashed potatoes (2 cups)

¼ cup all-purpose flour

2 eggs

½ teaspoon each salt and pepper

½ cup sharp cheddar cheese, shredded

¼ cup green onion, diced

½ cup sour cream

4-6 slices of bacon, cooked and crumbled

Prepare potatoes according to package directions. In a large bowl, combine the mashed potatoes, flour, eggs, salt, pepper, cheese and onion and stir until blended. Place ¼ to ½ cup potato batter (depending on size of waffle iron) into the center of the waffle iron and close lid. Cook until golden brown, about 3-5 minutes. Top with sour cream and crumbled bacon.

1 package of fresh baby spinach

1 pint fresh strawberries, sliced

½ cup Candied Pecans

4 ounces feta cheese, crumbled

4-6 slices bacon, cooked & crumbled

Poppy Seed Dressing

In a large bowl, toss all ingredients with 4-6 tablespoons of dressing or until coated to your preference.

Candied Pecans

See page 163

Poppy Seed Dressing

¼ cup white wine vinegar

¼ cup sugar

1 tablespoon poppy seeds

1 teaspoon ground mustard

1 teaspoon mayonnaise

½ cup olive oil

In a small bowl, whisk together vinegar and sugar until the sugar is mostly dissolved. Add the poppy seeds, ground mustard and mayonnaise and whisk to combine. Continue to whisk while slowly adding in olive oil. Transfer to a covered dish or Mason jar and store in refrigerator for up to 2 weeks. Dressing will separate as it sits. Shake before serving.

Chocolate Cinnamon Rolls Topped with Cream Cheese Icing

1 package refrigerated pizza crust

¼ cup Nutella

2 tablespoons butter, melted

¼ cup white sugar

¼ cup brown sugar

1 tablespoon ground cinnamon

Preheat oven to 375 degrees. Unroll pizza crust and spread evenly with Nutella and melted butter, in that order. Sprinkle remaining ingredients evenly across all of the dough. Roll up dough lengthwise and slice into 1 inch thick rolls. Place on a greased 9 x 9-inch pan and bake for 15 minutes. Place Cream Cheese Icing in a resealable bag, cut one corner and pipe onto cinnamon rolls.

Cream Cheese Icing

8 tablespoons (1 stick) butter, softened

1 (8 ounce) package cream cheese

1 teaspoon vanilla extract

3 cups powdered sugar

In a large bowl, using a hand mixer, combine butter, cream cheese, and vanilla until blended. Add powdered sugar one cup at a time until all 3 cups are blended.

Blackberry Bread Pudding

I French loaf

1 tablespoon butter

2 cups fresh blackberries

8 eggs

3 cups milk

1 cup heavy cream

2 cups sugar

1 teaspoon vanilla extract

1 teaspoon cinnamon

1 teaspoon nutmeg

Cut the French loaf into ½ inch cubes. Coat the bottom and sides of a 9 x 13-inch baking dish with butter. Place the cubes of bread and blackberries in the dish, distributing evenly. In a large bowl, whisk together the remaining ingredients and pour over bread and blackberries. Cover and refrigerate for at least 1 hour to overnight. Preheat oven to 350 degrees. Bake for 30 minutes covered with foil and 30 minutes uncovered. It should still be a little "jiggly" in the middle. Allow to cool for 15 minutes before serving.

Southwest Quiche

1 9-inch refrigerated pie crust

1 (8.5 ounce) can black beans, drained

1 (8.5 ounce) can corn

½ cup frozen spinach, thawed and drained

1 can Ro-tel

¼ cup green onion, chopped

1 teaspoon cumin

1 teaspoon chili powder

1 teaspoon cayenne pepper (optional)

1 teaspoon each salt and pepper

2 cups Colby/Monterey cheese, shredded

8 eggs

1 cup milk

Preheat oven to 350 degrees. Roll out pie crust and place in a 9-inch pie dish. Trim the extra crust off the sides and crimp with a fork. In a large bowl, combine the black beans, corn, spinach, Ro-tel, green onion, cumin, chili powder, cayenne powder, salt and pepper. Place half of the mixture in the pie dish and top with one cup of cheese. Add remaining filling and top with the remaining cup of cheese. In a large bowl, whisk together the eggs and milk and pour over the ingredients in the pie dish. Bake for 1 hour or until a toothpick inserted in the middle comes out clean. Allow to cool for 10 minutes before serving. If the crust begins to brown too much while baking, cover the edges with foil.

Fried Glazed Donuts

¾ cup milk

¼ cup oil

1 egg

1 teaspoon sugar

1 teaspoon vanilla extract

3 cups all-purpose flour

1 tablespoon baking powder

6 cups oil for frying

In a large bowl, stir together the milk, oil, egg, sugar and vanilla extract. Slowly stir in the flour and baking powder until dough forms. On a lightly floured surface, roll out the dough until it is ½ inch thick. Using a cup, cookie cutter or biscuit cutter, cut out the donuts. Then, using a small glass or cookie cutter, cut out the center hole. Heat oil in a deep fryer or Dutch oven to 350 degrees. Fry each donut and donut hole for 1-2 minutes or until golden brown, flipping once. Remove from oil and drain on paper towels. Dip in Glaze and serve.

Glaze

2 cups powdered sugar

¼ cup milk

In a medium bowl, stir together ingredients until well blended.

Here is another topping option for the donuts:

Cinnamon Sugar Topping

½ cup sugar

1 teaspoon cinnamon

In a large resealable bag, combine the sugar and cinnamon. Add 2 donuts at a time to the bag then seal and shake to coat.

SATURDAY
WILL VS. EVERYONE - GAME STARTS @ NOON
WILL & MEG'S PLACE

Will

"You're going down, Montgomery," Jules, my sister, yells out from across the yard, pointing her pink-tipped nail at me and glaring like we're in the middle of the fourth quarter of the Super Bowl.

"Yeah?" I walk toward her, strutting a bit. "Who's taking me down?"

"Me," she says, punches me in the arm, and jogs away, leaving me scowling after her.

"You're a brat!"

She sticks her tongue out at me as she assumes her position in the line.

It's one of the last weekends of the summer, so Meg and I invited the family over to spend time in the pool, play some ball, and just enjoy each other for the day.

"Where are the kids?" I hear Sam ask as she and Leo arrive. She strips her bathing suit cover-up off, then jumps in the pool with Meg and Natalie.

Everyone else is playing football on the lawn.

"They're all with the grandparents," Meg replies. "Today is adults only."

"Okay, let's do this," Caleb says, rubbing his hands together. He's the quarterback on his team, and of all things, I'm playing defense.

It's fun as fuck.

The ball is snapped, and we all start running around in a flurry. I'm holding back Matt, who just smirks, pushes back on my chest, and easily runs past me.

All of my brothers should have been professional athletes.

Caleb throws the ball, and Matt catches it, running it in for a touchdown.

"Yes!" Jules yells, high-fiving Matt.

And so it goes for the next thirty minutes, most of the siblings, including their spouses, playing football in the warm Seattle sunshine.

"That's enough," Brynna says at last, breathing hard. "I need food, something to drink, and a swim. Not in that order."

"Half time," I announce and jog over to the full spread of food that Meg had catered this morning. I grab a plate, and heap it high with chicken teriyaki pop things, buffalo chicken sliders, chips with a corn dip, and po' boys, too. I carry my bounty to a lounge chair and sit happily, watching my gorgeous girl floating in the water as I set out to fill my belly. "You should join us for the second half," I suggest to Meg.

She smiles and shakes her head. "I'm happy here in the pool. It's too hot to sweat like that."

"You can always get back in the pool."

But I can see by the look on her face that she's not interested in playing.

"That's fine, be a lazy bones over there."

"I intend to," she says with a wink and then turns her attention back to Natalie and Sam. Luke wades out with them, and kisses his wife as if they're still dating and all by themselves, per usual for them. Jules wrinkles her nose.

"Seriously? Ew. Get a fucking room."

"No," Luke replies with a smug smile. "Go kiss on your husband if you're jealous."

"I'm not jealous," she replies with a sigh. "It's just... ew."

We laugh, and I survey the pool area, soaking it all in. Once football season starts for me next week, I'll be gone more than I'm home, and I'll miss a lot of family gatherings. If our parents instilled anything in us, it was that family is the most important thing. No matter who you are, or what you do, it isn't worth anything if you don't have your family by your side.

And something we've learned as the years have progressed is that family comes in several forms. It's not always blood. It's who you trust, who you love, and who you can't imagine not being part of your life.

"Hey everyone," Dominic says as he and his wife, Alecia, walk into the back yard. "Sorry we're late. We got hung up in Saturday Seattle traffic."

"We're just glad you made it," Isaac says as he gives them both a hug.

Speaking of crazy family ties. None of us even knew that our brother, Dominic, existed until about five years ago. We weren't sure about him at first, but now I can't imagine not having him in my life. He's as much my brother as Caleb, Isaac or Matt.

"Come get some food! Good God, these antipasto cups are amazing," Jules says, happily munching next to me.

"Are Wyatt and Lia coming today?" Nic asks as she nibbles on the corn dip and chips. Man, I need to get me some more of that.

"I don't think so," Meg replies. "I think they're all at a birthday party today. And speaking of missing in action, where are Mark and Mer?"

"Lucy wasn't feeling well," Stacy says. Lucy is Mark and Meredith's two-year-old daughter. "I think she has a horrible summer cold."

"Poor little baby," Meg says, sticking her lower lip out.

I want to bite that lip. Jesus, she's fucking beautiful.

"Did you see that these strawberries have been soaked in champagne?" Stacy asks as she joins us, Isaac not far behind her. "They're heaven on a plate. It's such a good idea."

"Seriously?" Jules leans over to take a bite of one of Stacy's berries. "Oh my God, so good. I'm going to go get some." She jumps up and jogs over to the table, loading up on more food.

"Don't get drunk on those berries! I still have to beat your ass in the second half," I call out. She just flips me the bird.

Yeah, family days are the fucking best.

"Good God, look at this spread," Alecia says. "I'm starving. And it looks like I'd better get this caterer's name from you as well, just in case. Between the engagement party last week and this one, I need an extra three hours at the gym every day."

"No, you don't," Dom says, kissing her temple. "Eat whatever you want."

Alecia blushes as she reaches for the delicious bacon cheeseburger thingies. Yeah, I need to get me some more of those.

"We always eat well," Sam says as she climbs out of the pool, wraps a towel around her waist, and walks over to the buffet. "Leo, do you want some food?"

The rock star is lounging in a chair, his sunglasses on, a beer in his hand, watching his wife from across the pool.

"I'll eat off of your plate," he says, making Sam roll her eyes.

"I'm getting two of everything then, because I'm hungry and this spread is something to write home about. Oh, God, there's margarita cheesecake bites for dessert."

"I gave Nic the weekend off from baking," Meg says, sending a wink to Nic, who just shrugs.

"I would have brought some cupcakes. It's not a big deal."

"You deserve a day off, too," I reply.

We're always hungry. Okay, so I'm always hungry. I could eat everything on that table by myself.

I have a crazy fast metabolism, and I work my ass off pretty much every day, so I need more calories.

And my family never fails to give me shit about it, which is fine. As long as they keep feeding me.

Meg also climbs out of the pool and sits on the edge of my chair, dripping water on me. I don't care in the least.

"If you eat all of these chicken teriyaki things, there won't be enough for everyone else."

I narrow my eyes on her, then set my plate aside, pick her up, and unceremoniously throw her in the pool.

"Hey!"

"You clearly needed to cool off. You're getting a little salty."

She sputters, pushing her red hair out of her face, and then she just starts to laugh, that full-on belly laugh that never fails to make me weak in the knees.

I have it bad for this woman. Thank God she agreed to marry me.

I return to my food, and slip into an easy conversation with Matt and Caleb about sports.

"Speaking of touchdowns, let's do this," I say and lead everyone back out to the lawn. It's getting hotter now that the sun is high above us, but we have a cool breeze coming off the Sound.

"What's the score?" Isaac asks.

"Fourteen to six, we're winning," Jules announces with a triumphant smile. "I know, you're not used to losing, but you're going to be okay."

"I'm going to drop kick you into next week." I glare at her, but it has no effect on her whatsoever. She knows I'm a pushover.

"Right." She smirks, then leans in to kiss Nate on the shoulder. "I like it when you wear a tank top."

"Do you?" he asks, securing his hair at the back of his neck.

"Yeah. You don't often. You're usually all suited up. I like seeing your tattoos."

"If you're done flirting with your husband, we can get this game going."

She just smiles happily and walks to her place in the line. One thing's for sure, my baby sister is a pain in my ass.

And probably my best friend in the world, outside of Meg.

We play for the next ten minutes without either team scoring. There are some choice words between Nate and Matt, but then they start to laugh and all is well again.

But on the next play, Luke throws the ball to me, and I catch it, but when I turn to run with it, I twist the fuck out of my knee and fall.

Hard.

Shit.

"Time's up," Jules announces with a happy little dance. "We won!"

"Yeah, yeah," I mutter and cringe when I straighten my knee. Damn it. Not that I'll let anyone else see that it's killing me, but it hurts. Our first game is next week. I can't have an injury.

So, I stand, walk without limping, which is a huge undertaking by the way, but I'm used to it because I do it almost every week for the TV cameras. I approach the food table for another buffalo slider, and make it look like nothing's wrong.

Meg is watching me with concerned brown eyes, but I just shrug and throw her a confident smile that I don't necessarily feel all the way to my core. I need a break from prying eyes, and to evaluate just how much damage I've done.

"I'll be right back," I say with a quick wave and walk inside, through our house, dodging little girl toys on my way to our bedroom.

I walk right into the bathroom and sit on the toilet seat, extending and contracting my leg, taking stock of how much damage I just did.

I'm sure I didn't tear anything. I've had that happen before, and it hurts like a sonofabitch. No, I twisted it. It'll swell, but it'll recover in a few days If I stay off of it and ice it.

I hope.

I reach for some Icy Hot and rub it into the joint, and the muscles around it, sighing as it starts to work a little magic.

I stand to wash my hands, and then rub my wet hands over my face. Looking at myself in the mirror, I sigh deeply.

I injure far easier than I did when I was younger. And let's be honest, I've been lucky. With only two concussions and one dislocation on my medical resume, I know that it could be far, far worse.

But that's just it. I don't want to get to a point in my career where I'm forced to quit because of injuries. Not only is it easier to get hurt these days, but it takes me twice as long to heal. And it hurts far worse than it ever used to. Now I know what they mean when they say I'm too old for this shit.

I'm not twenty-five anymore. I'm staring down at my late thirties, and I'm grateful that I've had football for this long.

Most don't.

Hell, 99% don't.

I want to have time to enjoy my family. Erin will be small for such a short amount of time. I feel like I've already missed so much as my nieces and nephews have grown up.

I'm sick of missing everything.

Family comes first.

I stare at my reflection for another moment and then sigh, finally admitting what's been right in front of me for the past two years.

"Maybe it's time."

Meg

I love having the family over. I don't care that it's a lot of work. I did it right this time and hired the caterer, as well as asked my housekeeper to come yesterday to get everything spruced up so I didn't have to.

Chasing after a baby is exhausting. She's still little, but she's demanding and sometimes everything is just plain overwhelming.

So I've learned how to ask for help, and that's made a huge difference.

Because I'm not gonna lie. I'm damn exhausted.

I walk over and plop down in the chair next to Leo and Sam, crossing my ankles and resting my arm over my head.

"Hey." I smile over at them. "How are you guys?"

"We're great," Leo replies, taking a bite of Sam's food. "How are you?"

"Fine."

Leo takes his glasses off and watches me with narrowed blue eyes, making me frown.

"What? I'm fine."

"You look tired."

"Thanks. I think that's the same as saying you look like shit."

"That's not what I said."

"It's kind of the same thing," Sam agrees, nodding as she chews on a champagne-soaked berry. Damn, I wish I could eat some of those.

"Whose side are you on, sunshine?"

"No sides," Sam replies with a laugh. "I'm just agreeing with Meg."

"Yeah, taking her side," Leo says and slaps Sam on the ass, making her jump and her cheeks turn pink at the same time.

"Don't start something you can't finish, Leo Nash."

He grins at her, then turns back to me. "So tell me what's going on."

"Oh my God." I sigh in exasperation. "There is nothing going on."

"I know you," he reminds me. And he does. He's the closest thing I have to a brother, and I love him like crazy.

Even though he drives me crazy.

"Leave her alone," Sam says. "Do you think you can get a sitter for Erin Thursday night?"

"I'm sure I can. What's up?"

Leo grins as Sam eats another berry.

"The band's coming up from L.A. and we're going to have dinner at our place," Leo says. "We'd love for you and Will to come. Bring your guitar. We're going to write some songs."

"Why don't you look excited about this?" I ask Sam, who won't look Leo in the face as she bites her lip.

"I'm excited."

Leo and I exchange a look. "Yeah, I can clearly see this is your super excited face."

She laughs and tucks her hair behind her ear. "Leo promised after the last world tour that he would take some time off. Having the guys up to start writing songs just a few months later isn't really taking time off."

"I told you, we aren't recording. We don't have anything planned for the foreseeable future."

She nods, but doesn't look convinced.

"When you're in a band, it's like being part of a close family," I begin, hoping to give her some new perspective. "We know how that is. You spend weeks, sometimes months with the same people, day in and day out. And then, when the tour is over, you all go your separate ways, and you feel a little lost."

"Do you feel lost?" Sam asks Leo, dragging her fingertips down his cheek.

"I want to see them," he replies as he shrugs one shoulder. "Writing a few songs doesn't mean we're going back out on the road next week."

She sighs, and then smiles. "I know. I'm just selfish with your down time."

"I get it, trust me." I reach over and give her hand a pat. "I live for the off season when Will isn't traveling with the team all the time. He's good about making sure the turn around time is short, but it's still demanding."

Sam nods and offers me a happy smile. "Thanks."

"I'd love to come see the guys," I continue. "I've started writing a few songs, but haven't finished anything. Maybe you can help me."

"You're writing again?" Leo's smile is wide. "Since when?"

"Since I was pregnant with Erin. The hormones made me creative, and I started several pieces."

"I'm excited to hear them," he replies.

My stomach growls, making me scowl. I just had two sliders not even thirty minutes ago. "I'm going to go find food."

I stand and walk away, tired and hungry, and resigned to this being my lot in life for the next nine or so months.

Not that it's a bad lot in life. Not at all.

As I walk past the pool, it occurs to me that I haven't seen Will in a while. Maybe he went inside?

I pass the food and head indoors, walking through the living room and stepping over Erin's things. I should have picked them up this morning, but I was too tired, and not a little nervous about the news I'd just received.

I wander back to our room and find Will in the bathroom, leaning on the sink and breathing deeply. His shoulders are so damn broad, his dark blond hair longer than usual. His back narrows to a tight waist and the sexiest ass this side of the Mississippi.

Or that side, for that matter.

"Are you okay?" That gets his attention. He whirls around and takes me in, from head to toe, the way he always does when I walk into a room.

It just never gets old.

A slow smile slips over his lips as he advances toward me.

"I'm great."

"I saw you fall earlier. Do you need help?"

"It's nothing."

But something in his eyes shuts down, sending off warning bells. Before I can ask him about it, he walks me backwards toward our bed.

"Will, we have more than a dozen people out at our pool."

"Exactly." He shuts and locks the door, and walks toward me, his blue eyes hot with lust, and everything else completely escapes my head. "They're out at the pool, and none of them cares where we are."

"They might come looking for us."

He slowly climbs over me on the bed, pinning me beneath him. He fists his hands in my damp hair and kisses me for all he's worth.

And trust me when I say he's worth a lot.

His tongue slides along mine in an ancient rhythm of lust and love, and I am helpless to do anything but hold on to the waistband of his swim trunks and enjoy the ride he's decided to take us on.

God bless him.

"You're so fucking sexy," he murmurs against my lips as his hand glides up my bare skin. "But I need to get you out of this bikini."

"Be my guest," I purr, and watch in fascination as his eyes dilate.

He pulls the string at my hips, and the bottoms fall away, then he does the same to the top. I'm naked in one-point-six seconds flat, and Will's mouth is on my breast, gently sucking my already hard nipple.

He learned with the last pregnancy to be gentle with my nipples, and he hasn't grown out of the habit, thank God. His hand travels from my other breast down my belly to my sensitive core, where he lightly flicks my piercing back and forth, making me practically come out of my damn skin.

"Will, my God."

"I'll never get enough of you," he growls. He's leaving open-mouthed kisses over my skin on his way south, and when he plants that magical mouth on my clit, I swear to Jesus, I see stars.

My hips buck, giving him the perfect opportunity to slide his hands under my ass, holding me up so he can feast on me.

And feast on me he does, until everything is a kaleidoscope of bright color and I'm freefalling through the craziest orgasm I've had in months.

Before I can catch my breath, Will kisses his way up my side, then slips easily inside me. I'm so fucking wet, I'll have to change the bed later, and I don't give even one fuck.

Sex with Will gets better every time.

And how, exactly, is that possible?

He flips us easily, steadying me over him, and I happily ride him until we're both gasping for breath and he sits up, wraps his arms around me, and succumbs to his own orgasm.

I brush his hair off of his forehead and kiss him softly.

"Always so good," I murmur.

"God, I love you, Megan. More every day."

I smile, my heart expanding with gratitude and love for this man.

"I love you, too."

I wasn't always able to say that. It frustrated the hell out of both of us. But now, I say it every chance I get because he deserves to hear it a million times a day.

He gently lifts me off him, and then we set to work getting redressed and cleaned up.

"Megan."

"Hmm?" I glance up to find him staring at me with serious blue eyes. "What is it?"

He sighs, his hands on his hips. "What would you say if I told you that I think it's almost time that I retire?"

Holy shit.

I do a happy dance.

I scream YES!

I cry and thank God.

All in my head.

"Well, you know that I'll always support anything you decide when it comes to your career."

And it's true. I will. Because I love him, and he would always do the same for me. He has done the same. I didn't want to be a stay-at-home mom, even though we could definitely afford for me to be. I love my job as a nurse at Seattle Children's, and when Erin was three months old, Will completely supported my decision to go back to work and hire a nanny.

He didn't even bat an eye.

So how can I be anything but supportive in return?

"Tell me what you really think."

"I just did," I reply. "I will honestly support any decision that you make. If you want to retire after this season, I'll be fine with it. If you want to play for five more years, I'll be good with that, too."

But I'll worry, every single day. I see the toll football is taking on his body. I know that even Will Montgomery can't sustain this forever.

But it absolutely has to be his decision.

"We'll talk about it more, but I'm leaning toward this being my last season."

He rubs his hand over his mouth, as if he can't believe that he just said it aloud. I hurry to him and wrap my arms around his waist, lay my head on his chest and hug him close.

"I love you so much. You're an amazing football player, Will. Nothing will ever change that."

"Yeah. I just want to go out on my terms, you know?"

I nod and smile up at him. "I get it."

"Let's not talk about it with the family yet. I still need to talk to my agent and the organization before we make any concrete decisions."

I push up on my tiptoes, offering him my lips. "Thank you for including me in this decision."

"You and Erin are my life, Megan. You're the most important."

I feel tears prick my eyes, and I bury my face in his chest again, take a deep breath, and tell him what I've been dying to say all day.

"I know that the three of us would prefer you were with us more."

He pauses, then grips my shoulders and pushes me back to look me in the eyes.

"The three of you?"

I nod and swallow hard. "I found out this morning, I'm pregnant again."

His jaw drops, making me giggle.

"I know Erin is still so small, and these babies will be close together, but it looks like the unexpected happened," I continue, and I suddenly find myself lifted into the air, and he's stomping through the house to the pool. "Don't tell everyone. I'm only about five weeks along. Anything could happen."

"Fuck that," he growls. "I'm telling everyone."

He marches outside, and dozens of eyes turn to us.

"I have an announcement," Will says. "We're going to have another baby!"

Chaos ensues. Will's brothers all rush over to boost me onto their shoulders, as if I just saved the game with the winning run.

It's weird, but it's funny, so whatever.

I'm finally put on my feet, and all of the girls immediately surround me with questions and hugs and not a few tears.

"Here," Will says, interrupting. "Let's get her a seat in the shade."

"I'm fine."

He glares at me, making me laugh. I shrug and sit in a shady spot, and Jules, Nat, Stacy, Brynna, Sam, Nic and Alecia join me.

The guys are laughing and high-fiving, and I can't help but roll my eyes.

"They're cavemen."

"Oh yeah," Nat agrees, nodding. "But they're the best kind of cavemen."

"A second baby, so soon," Jules says. "Oh, my heart."

"And oh, my body," I reply with a groan. "This wasn't planned. And Nic, please don't be offended. I know you—"

"Stop," Nic says, holding up her hand. "I'm great. In fact, Matt and I will be adding to our family soon."

Jules smiles and the rest of our jaws drop. "Well, we clearly need more information," I say.

"Nope, this is all about you," Nic replies. "And you don't have to worry about me."

"I'm sure it was a surprise," Sam says.

"Shocker of the year," I agree. "I mean, I'm all for having another baby, but Erin will be barely a year old when this one comes."

"You'll get through it," Natalie assures me, just as Will arrives with a plate of food, making my stomach growl again.

"I don't have broken legs," I remind him. "I can get my own food."

"It's pamper time, Megan," he says with a wink, then returns to chat with his brothers.

"Cavemen," I mutter again, but Alecia shakes her head.

"Do you know how many women out there wish they had a guy who treated them half as well as ours do us? Trust me, I work with women, and it's a lot. I'd say we're pretty lucky."

I smile as I watch Will glance my way, wink, and then reply to something Nate just said.

"I never dared dream I'd be so lucky," I reply softly. "Honestly, you guys. This is more than my imagination could have come up with."

"Same," Sam says with a grin. Her voice is gruffer than usual, as she blinks away tears. "I may not want babies of my own, but I sure am grateful that y'all keep popping them out so I can spoil them like crazy."

"We're happy to oblige," Jules says with a laugh. "Wow, so many babies and weddings happening these days. A lot can change in five years."

"A lot can change in five minutes," I reply. "One minute, Will was blissfully unaware that he was about to be a daddy again, and the next? Pow."

"It's going to be awesome," Sam assures me.

"You won't have two babies in diapers."

She frowns. "Thank God."

I take a deep breath. I can do this.

Of course I can.

Look who I have at my back. Not just Will, but all of these wonderful people.

We can't lose.

GAME DAY

LOLLIPOP CHICKEN WITH SESAME TERIYAKI GLAZE

BACON CHEESEBURGER PINWHEELS

BUFFALO CHICKEN SLIDERS WITH RANCH SLAW

SPICY CORN DIP WITH HOMEMADE CHIPS

SHRIMP PO' BOYS

TIPSY BERRIES

ANTIPASTO CUPS

MARGARITA CHEESECAKE BITES

12 chicken wing drumsticks

1 teaspoon salt

1 teaspoon pepper

6 cups oil

Heat oil in a Dutch oven or deep fryer to 350 degrees. To make the "lollipop," take the drumstick part of the chicken wing and make a cut completely to the bone around the entire bottom of the drumstick. Push the meat down to the large end. Season the chicken with salt and pepper. Fry chicken in oil until crisp and internal temp is 165 degrees, 8-10 minutes. Remove from oil and drain on paper towels. Place chicken in a large bowl and cover with Sesame Teriyaki Glaze. Toss to cover and serve.

Sesame Teriyaki Glaze

½ cup soy sauce

¼ cup water

2 tablespoons rice wine vinegar

2 tablespoons brown sugar

2 tablespoons honey

¼ cup sugar

1 teaspoon minced garlic

1 teaspoon ground ginger

2 tablespoons cold water

1 tablespoon cornstarch

¼ cup sesame seeds

In a small saucepan over low heat, combine all ingredients except the cold water and cornstarch. Stir constantly until sugar dissolves, about 2-3 minutes. Increase temperature to medium high. In a small bowl, stir together the cold water and cornstarch. Stir the cornstarch into the soy mixture and simmer for 1 minute or until thickened. Remove from heat and stir in sesame seeds.

Bacon Cheeseburger Pinwheels

1 pound ground beef

6 slices bacon, diced

1 small onion, diced

8 ounces Velveeta cheese, cut into 1-inch cubes

1 refrigerated pizza crust

1 cup Thousand Island dressing

½ cup dill pickle slices

1 tablespoon melted butter

2 cups shredded lettuce

2 tomatoes, chopped

Preheat oven to 400 degrees. In a large skillet over medium heat, brown the ground beef, bacon and onion. Drain off grease and return meat mixture to the skillet. Reduce heat to low and add Velveeta cheese to the skillet. Stir until the cheese is melted and blended together, about 5 minutes. Remove from heat and cool completely. Unroll pizza crust dough onto a greased cookie sheet, spreading to cover the entire sheet. Spread the dressing over the entire surface. Place the pickle slices down one of the long sides and top with the meat mixture. Roll up, starting at the long side with the filling. Move to the center of the cookie sheet and brush the top with butter. Bake for 20-25 minutes or until golden brown. Slice and serve with additional dressing, lettuce and tomato.

Buffalo Chicken Sliders with Ranch Slaw

6 cups oil

4 boneless skinless chicken breasts

4 cups flour

1 tablespoon seasoning salt

2 cups milk

1 cup hot sauce

8 tablespoons (1 stick) butter, melted

1 teaspoon garlic powder

1 tablespoon Worcestershire sauce

24 Hawaiian rolls

Heat oil in a deep fryer or Dutch oven to 350 degrees. Cut the chicken breasts into 3 pieces and pound out flat by placing the chicken in a resealable bag and pounding with a rolling pin until ½ inch thick. Mix together the flour and seasoning salt in a large bowl. Pour milk in a separate bowl. Place the chicken in the flour, then in the milk and then again in the flour mixture. Place 2 pieces of chicken in the oil and fry until golden brown, about 4-6 minutes. Remove from oil and drain on a paper towel. Repeat with remaining chicken. In a large bowl, combine the hot sauce, butter, garlic powder and Worcestershire sauce. Dip each piece of chicken in the sauce and set aside.

Ranch Slaw

1 package tri-color slaw

Homemade Ranch Dressing

Combine the slaw with the Homemade Ranch Dressing and refrigerate for at least 1 hour.

Homemade Ranch Dressing

½ cup mayonnaise

¼ cup sour cream

2 tablespoons milk

¼ teaspoon dried chives

¼ teaspoon dried parsley

¼ teaspoon dried dill weed

¼ teaspoon garlic powder

¼ teaspoon onion powder

Pinch of salt and pepper

Add all ingredients to a Mason jar and shake well. Refrigerate for up to a week.

To prepare the sliders:

Place all 24 rolls out flat and remove top bun. Top with chicken* to cover all of the bread and then top with slaw. Place remaining buns on top of slaw and separate into 24 sliders.

*The chicken will cover 2 buns each.

Spicy Corn Dip with Homemade Chips

1 (15.5 ounce) can white corn

1 (15.5 ounce) can yellow corn

8 ounces cream cheese

1 cup mayonnaise

1 cup grated Parmesan cheese

1 tablespoon garlic powder

½ cup green onion, chopped

¼ cup fresh jalapeno, chopped (seeds removed)

1 teaspoon salt

1 teaspoon pepper

1 teaspoon cayenne pepper

2 cups cheddar cheese, shredded

1 tablespoon red pepper flakes

Preheat oven to 350 degrees. In a large bowl, mix together all of the ingredients except for 1 cup of the cheddar cheese and red pepper flakes. Place in a baking dish and top with remaining cheddar cheese. Bake for 30 minutes. Remove from oven and top with red pepper flakes. Serve immediately with Homemade Chips.

Homemade Chips

5 baking potatoes, peeled

4 cups oil

3-4 tablespoons seasoning salt

Slice potatoes with a mandolin on the thinnest setting or slice thinly with a knife. Heat oil to 350 degrees in a Dutch oven or deep fryer. Cook potatoes in 5 different batches for about 2 minutes each, being careful not to overcrowd. Sprinkle each batch with seasoning salt immediately after removing from oil.

Shrimp Po' Boys

6 cups oil

2 eggs

1 cup milk

2 cups flour

1 cup cornmeal

1 tablespoon Cajun seasoning

1 pound (21-30 count) shrimp, peeled and deveined

1 teaspoon salt

1 teaspoon pepper

4 tablespoons melted butter

8 hoagie buns, split

Remoulade Sauce

Leaf lettuce

Sliced tomatoes

1 lemon

Heat oil to 375 degrees. In a small bowl, whisk together the eggs and milk. In a separate bowl, mix together 1 cup of flour, cornmeal and Cajun seasoning. In a third bowl, add the remaining flour. Season the shrimp with salt and pepper. Dredge about 10 shrimp at a time in the plain flour, then the egg mixture, and finally in the flour/cornmeal mixture. Shake off the excess and place in deep fryer. Fry for 1 to 2 minutes or until shrimp are cooked through. Continue with remaining shrimp and place on paper towels to drain. Spread butter on the inside of the buns and toast in the oven. Spread Remoulade Sauce on both sides of the bread, add 3-5 shrimp and top with lettuce, sliced tomatoes and a squirt of juice from a lemon wedge.

Remoulade Sauce

1 cup mayo

3 tablespoons whole grain mustard

1 tablespoon extra hot horseradish

2 tablespoons lemon juice

2 teaspoons Cajun seasoning

1 teaspoon minced garlic

Mix all ingredients in a small bowl and refrigerate for at least an hour before serving.

Tipsy Berries

3 pints fresh strawberries, stems removed

2 cups champagne

½ cup vodka

1 cup sugar*

Place strawberries in a large bowl and cover with champagne and vodka. Cover and refrigerate for 1 hour. Drain strawberries in a colander. Roll in sugar and serve.

*Add ½ cup different color sugar sprinkles to the sugar to personalize for any occasion.

Antipasto Cups

12 slices salami

1 (15.5 ounce) can baby artichoke hearts, chopped

1 cup Kalamata olives, chopped

½ cup sliced banana peppers

1 (12 ounce) jar roasted red peppers, chopped

3 tablespoons olive oil

2 tablespoons red wine vinegar

1 teaspoon salt

1 teaspoon pepper

1 teaspoon garlic powder

1 cup feta cheese, crumbled

Preheat oven to 400 degrees. Press salami into 12 muffin cups and place a small ball of foil in the middle to hold in place. Bake for 5-7 minutes or until edges begin to brown. Remove from pan and place on paper towels to drain. In a large bowl, combine remaining ingredients except for feta cheese. Toss well. Place the salami cups on a platter and fill with antipasto mixture. Top with cheese and serve.

Margarita Cheesecake Bites

1 cup crushed pretzels

8 tablespoons (1 stick) butter, melted

2 tablespoons sugar

2 (8 ounce) blocks cream cheese, softened

1 cup powdered sugar

Juice and zest of 1 lime

1 tablespoon tequila

1 teaspoon vanilla extract

½ teaspoon salt

Line 12 cupcake tins with liners. In a large bowl, mix together pretzels, butter and sugar. Press an even layer of crushed pretzels into the bottom of each muffin tin using the back of a spoon. Refrigerate for 10-15 minutes. In a large bowl, using a hand mixer, beat cream cheese and powdered sugar until combined. Mix in remaining ingredients, reserving some of the zest for the topping. Spread evenly over pretzel crust and top with remaining lime zest. Freeze for 1 hour or until ready to serve. To make a full cheesecake, press an even layer of the pretzel mix on the bottom of a 9-inch spring form pan. Refrigerate for 10-15 minutes. Spread the cheesecake mixture over the pretzels and top with remaining lime zest. Freeze for 1 hour before serving.

ew message

To: Guys in the band and Meg

Cc: Sam

Bcc:

Subject: Jam Session

Hey Everyone —

It's been a few months. I'm sending the plane to LA to bring you to Seattle for the weekend. I have some song ideas to work through, and Sam's gonna feed you.

Come to my house, fuckers.

— Leo

Sam and Leo

Leo

"They're on the way here from the airport," I inform Sam, who's sitting at her vanity in our closet putting the finishing touches on her hair. "I just got a call from Gary."

"Okay." She sighs and stares at herself in the mirror. She seems to be having a silent conversation with herself. One that I'm not part of.

"What's on your pretty mind?" I ask as I walk up behind her and look at her reflection, resting my hands on her shoulders.

"Nothing." She runs her brush through her blonde locks, acting as if nothing at all is bothering her.

But I know my wife, and this isn't the nothing nothing tone. This is the something nothing tone, and I'm going to have to pry it out of her.

Which is fine by me because it'll involve skin-to-skin contact.

I drag my hands from her shoulders to her elbows and kiss the top of her head, breathing in strawberries and vanilla, and watching her eyes widen and dilate in the mirror. Her cheeks flush, and her pink lips part as her breathing grows ragged.

"You know." I sweep her soft blonde hair to the side and kiss her neck, just below her ear. "I need you to talk to me, Sunshine."

"I don't have anything to say." Her raspy voice catches on "say" as I grip her earlobe in my teeth and give it a little pull. She tips her head, giving me easier access to her neck, which I take full advantage of, licking and kissing lightly.

It's about to get interesting.

She sighs, settling into my soft touches, so I fist her hair at the back of her head, catching her attention, and plant my teeth in the supple skin at the base of her neck where it meets the shoulder, and her breath immediately comes faster.

"You like it a little rough."

"Mm" is her only response, which always makes my dick twitch. I fucking love her raspy voice.

I pull her shirt and bra to the side, giving me more access to her, and leave open-mouthed kisses over her skin, which pebbles in goose bumps. Her breasts lift with her gasp, begging for my hands.

"You like that?" I whisper as I cup her tits and worry the already tight nipples between my finger and thumb.

"You know I like that."

I grin and bite her again, then nibble over to her spine.

Sam's back is fucking gorgeous.

"Take this off." I yank her shirt over her head and drop it on the floor, squat and kiss my way down her spine to the top of her ass.

"Oh, that's nice."

"Nice?" I lick the dimples above her ass. "This is nice?"

"It's good."

She giggles, but I drag my fingers up her sides, over her ribs, squashing her laughter and making her sigh again.

"Just good?"

"Okay, it's fucking amazing."

"That's what I want to hear."

My hands roam up her belly to her breasts again, teasing her over her bra.

"Talk to me," I murmur against her skin. "What's up with you?"

She sighs, leaning into me. "I don't want this weekend to be the beginning of a new surprise album and tour, Leo."

"That's not what we're doing." I turn her to face me and pull her into my arms. "We're just hanging out. I haven't seen them in a couple of months, and I miss their ugly faces."

She laughs and presses a kiss over my heart. "Okay."

The doorbell rings and I smile down at her. "They're here."

"Don't leave. You're not done with me yet."

I kiss her, hard, and then smile as I pull away. "I have to get it. We haven't hired a butler."

"Nor will we. Okay, go get it. I have to fix myself after your attack on me."

"You loved it," I toss over my shoulder as I jog through the house to the front door and open it wide, excited to see my band.

"Hello, darling," Cher, DJ's wife and a longtime friend of mine, says as she steps inside and kisses my cheek. "I have to use the bathroom."

She hurries down the hall as the rest file in, and Meg and Will pull up in Will's Mustang, just in time.

"It was a bumpy flight," Gary says after shaking my hand. "I've never been so glad to see land."

"Gary's a pussy," Eric replies.

"Motion sickness doesn't make me a pussy," Gary insists.

They're all here. Gary with his wife, Lori, Jake and Eric, who have both managed to stay single all these years, and DJ and Cher.

Meg and Will come up the front steps, Will carrying Meg's guitar for her.

"Looks like we have good timing," Meg says with a grin. "Hey, everyone!"

"Meg!"

She's immediately swept up amongst the guys, the way she always has been where they're concerned.

"Is there food?" Will asks, making me grin.

"Hungry already?"

"I had training today," he explains.

"That means nothing. You're always hungry," Sam says as she joins us and slips her arm around my waist. "But yes, we have tons of food. I had a caterer bring in a great assortment, all set up in the kitchen and dining room."

"Sweet." Will takes off for the kitchen, making us all laugh.

"It's so nice out today," Sam says after hugging and greeting everyone. "Let's sit outside."

"Your outdoor space should be in a magazine," Lori says as we grab drinks and some food and walk out back. We face the ocean, and Sam's right, it's a beautiful day for enjoying the view. It's a nice early fall day, and I set up the sun shades this morning.

"Thank you," Sam says. "You look fantastic for having a baby just a few months ago."

"Oh, thanks." Lori laughs and glances at her husband. Gary's still loading up a plate full of fried chicken and deviled eggs. "I think we're done with five."

"That's a lot of babies," Cher says as she walks outside with a bottle of water. "Who has them all this weekend?"

"My parents," Lori replies. "God bless them."

"You guys have to try these chicken kabob things," Jake says. "They're fucking amazing."

"I'm getting more ribs," Eric says, going back for round two of food.

"Go, before Will eats it all," Meg replies with a laugh, earning a glare from her husband, who's licking BBQ sauce off his fingers.

It's chaos for a while, as everyone chats and catches up on the past couple of months since we've seen each other.

"He needs a job," Lori says, pointing to Gary. "I swear, you guys come off tour, and he doesn't know what to do with himself. I'd be happy if he just volunteered somewhere."

"With five kids he should have plenty to do," Will says.

"They have their own routine," Gary says. "I don't mess with it much when I'm home because it just screws things up for her when I leave again."

"I get it," Cher says with a sigh. "But I'm glad you're home."

"Same," Sam says quietly and climbs into my lap, wrapping her arms around my neck. I know she hates it when I tour because I'm gone for so long, but it's part of the job.

DJ already has a guitar in his hands, randomly strumming. He starts playing the chords for a P!nk duet Sam and I love. She smiles down at me, and suddenly, to my utter shock, starts to sing.

Sam never sings in public, despite my urging her to. She says she leaves that to me.

But her voice is perfect for this song, and I join in on my parts, looking into her eyes as we sing in perfect harmony.

When the song is over we get a standing ovation, and Meg's shaking her head.

"Looks like I have competition and I didn't even know it."

"No," Sam replies. "Absolutely not. Leo and I play around here at home, but I don't sing in public."

"You should," Eric says. "You're fucking good."

"Leo's the musician in the family," she insists, patting my cheek and leaning in for a kiss. "Are you hungry?" she asks me.

"I am, actually."

"Want me to go get you something?"

"I'd love that, thank you." I cup her chin and kiss her once more before she hops off of my lap and I slap her ass.

"That's harassment," she calls over her shoulder as she walks away.

"You're welcome," I call back, making her laugh. The sound slides over my skin, making my gut clench.

God, I fucking love her.

"How's football going, Will?" Gary asks him.

"Good. It's early in the season yet, but the team is strong this year. Should be a good one. You'll have to come up sometime for a game. My family keeps a box and you're welcome to join them."

"That would be awesome," Lori says and claps her hands. "I love football."

"You're my kind of woman," Will says with a wink.

DJ is still strumming the guitar, something I don't recognize.

"What is that?" I ask him.

"Something I've been fiddling with," he replies. "I have some lyrics too, but I'm hung up on the bridge."

"Let's hear it," Jake says, eating some corn on the cob now. Sam delivers my plate, full of the corn, a burger, kabobs. If it's up there, she put it on my plate.

"Thanks, Sunshine. DJ's going to play something he's working on."

Her eyes flicker with something I can't name, but she smiles and sits next to me. "Cool."

The song is a ballad, about missing home and the woman who waits for him there.

"Again," Gary says, picking up his own guitar, and I take the lead while he and DJ sing harmony. In the third verse, Meg picks up a higher harmony, and the song sounds badass.

The others are chatting around us, eating food, and enjoying the day, but I'm lost in this song.

It's going to be a hit.

Before long, we've worked through the bridge, and have a complete song on our hands.

"This is fucking awesome," Jake says. "Let's go hit Leo's studio and record what we have."

"This isn't a working weekend, you guys," Cher reminds us all.

"You can't turn off the creative genius, baby," DJ replies with a wink, but Cher just glares at him.

"We won't forget this," I say. I can see the look on Sam's face, and it clearly says do not go record that song.

"I have some things that I've been working on, too," Meg says with a smile. "Since I had Erin, I've been full of creativity."

"Let's hear it," I say.

I haven't enjoyed an afternoon like this in a very long time. Jamming with the guys is like coming home. I think we all needed it because we're buzzing with energy by the time we finish fine-tuning one of Meg's songs.

"It's decided," DJ says with a grin. "Meg has to do a duet with us on the next album."

"I can't tour, guys," she insists. "I have a job and a kid. And a husband."

"You can prerecord your tracks and do a video for us to play at shows when you can't be there," Gary suggests. "People do that all the time."

"And then you can perform with us when we're in Seattle," I add. "You do it all the time anyway. Say yes."

She looks at Will, biting her lip. Will just shrugs and smiles at her. "It's totally up to you, Megan. You know I'm fine with it."

"We're a ways out before we start recording again," I remind her. "You don't have to decide today."

"Maybe we can talk Leo into hitting the studio earlier," Jake says. "I mean, we have half an album already, just from jamming today. There's no need to wait until next year."

"Except you promised your wives that you would take the year off," Cher says. Her eyes are flashing with annoyance.

"She's right." I shrug and set my guitar aside. "We did promise them. There's nothing wrong with taking a year off."

"It's boring," Eric replies.

"Go write for someone else," DJ suggests. "You write constantly. It doesn't mean that Nash has to record everything. You can sell your songs to other artists."

"You guys really wouldn't mind?" Eric asks. "I don't want to piss anyone off. My songs have always been for the band."

"Writing is your outlet," I reply. "There's no way we can possibly record all of the songs you write. You should sell them. Write all day every day if you want to."

Eric grins. "Okay, as long as you're sure. I've had some interest, but I didn't want to step on your toes. The band always comes first."

"Do it," Lori says. "Lots of musicians do this. David Bryan, the keyboardist for Bon Jovi? He writes music for Broadway. I say do whatever makes your heart happy."

"I don't want to do Broadway," Eric says. "But I'd like to write more."

"So let's talk about when we do go back out on tour," Jake says.

"Why?" Lori asks. "Can't you guys talk about anything else? Sports? Race cars? Gardening? Anything!"

"Gardening?" Eric snorts, but then narrows his eyes on Gary. "Does she have you gardening?"

"What?" Gary asks. "My yard looks damn good, thank you."

"He's a rockstar that's been voted one of the best of our generation, and his wife makes him mow the damn lawn," Jake says, shaking his head in disgust.

"What do you do with your off time?" Sam asks.

"Play video games, of course."

"I'm very good at video games," Meg says, but Will just rolls his eyes.

"She cheats."

"I do not."

"You do too."

"Whatever." Meg rolls her eyes. "Not that I have time to play them these days, but I am good at it. Will just doesn't like it because I beat him."

"Now that's a flat-out lie."

"Really." She cocks a brow and leans in to whisper something in his ear. Will smiles and shrugs a shoulder.

"Promises, promises."

"Hey, get a room," Sam says with a laugh.

"Seriously, Leo," DJ says, "let's go up and record this ballad. It's awesome just as it is. We could release it as a surprise single."

"It'll take ten minutes," Gary says.

"Okay, let's go. But just one song."

I glance to my right to tell Sam I'll be right back, but she's already gone, walking into the house.

Meg stands and runs after her.

Sam

I knew it.

I march into the kitchen and begin checking on the food, combining the last kabob on one plate onto a full plate of others and clearing it away.

Anything to get away from the conversation outside.

Meg walks in and shuts the door behind her.

"Are you okay?"

"Great." I drop a glass into the sink with a clunk. "Never better. Why do you ask?"

"Oh, I don't know, maybe because you look like you're ready to kill that chicken again, and it's already dead."

"You know, all I wanted was one year. Just one. No album releases, no tour, no special appearances. I wanted a year with my husband. And clearly that's just not going to happen because they're already writing songs and recording them."

"Sam, this is just what they do when they're together," Meg reminds me, but I shake my head.

"Maybe I was naïve to think that I could be married to a rock star."

"I think you're selling yourself short."

"Am I?" I wipe down the countertop, which was not dirty, by the way, then throw the sponge in the sink. "Because I've grown to hate it. And I used to love it."

"I'm telling you, they're having fun. They're catching up and enjoying each other. Making music is who they are when they're together, it doesn't mean that they're going to release an album or leave for tour next week. I've been around them for more than half my life. Trust me, this is normal."

"I know you're right." I lean on my hands and hang my head. "I've been dreading this weekend because it meant that I wouldn't have him to myself anymore, and I'd be sharing him with the people who always take him away from me. But they're his family too, and I need to remember that."

"Exactly. When you're with your family, you laugh and play around. That's all he's doing here."

"Thanks." I look up at her with a smile. "Thanks for putting it all into perspective for me. I needed that today."

"That's what I'm here for. Now, what's for dessert?"

"I have a lemon meringue pie and a s'mores trifle."

"Dear God, I love that you always have both lemon and chocolate around. It's not good for my waistline, but the sugar junky in me applauds you."

"Actually, let's take this stuff outside so everyone can have some."

I load up trays with the desserts, plates and utensils, and by the time we walk out with it all, Leo and the boys are back from the studio. Leo's changed out of his T-shirt into a loose tank that shows off all of his tattoos.

And although they're covered, I can't help but think of the stars that are on his hips, and how I want to trace them with my tongue later tonight.

"That was quick," I say, offering him some dessert.

"The song's easy." He takes the plate, but then snags his hand around my wrist and tugs me back into his lap. "Have I told you today that I love you?"

And just like that, I'm as mushy as I get.

"What do you want?"

"Just you." He plants a kiss on me. "Where did you go?"

"I wanted to check on the food and bring out dessert."

I don't mention my mini meltdown because it won't do any good. I don't want to start an argument with everyone here.

Especially one that I can't win.

I take a deep breath and try to shake my mood. I don't want the day to be ruined. So they talk about touring and music, as they should. It's their job.

I need to not take everything so personally and just enjoy my husband and his friends.

"Hey," Jake says with a laugh, "remember in Nashville when Eric brought those two chicks into the bus and fucked them both?"

And, queue uncomfortable silence.

"Which tour was that on?" Lori asks.

"That last one," Jake says. "We were in Nashville in what, February?"

"February," DJ says, avoiding eye contact with his wife, who's shooting daggers at him.

I'm watching Leo, but he has no reaction at all, just shakes his head.

"Wait," Lori says, holding up her hand. "You had women on your bus in February?"

"Yeah," Eric says with a sigh, then laughs at the memory. "Man, they were wild."

"No, this is not cool, Eric," Lori says. "We have a rule, a longstanding rule at that, that there are to be no women on the goddamn bus."

"Hey, I was drunk and we weren't near the hotel," he says, holding hands out at his side. "What was I supposed to do? The girls wanted me to show them a good time. And man did I."

"The one tried to climb in bed with Leo," Jake adds, and my gaze whips to my husband, who's still impassive.

"Wasn't it Nashville when I wasn't able to reach you?" I ask him. His eyes turn to mine, and his whole body goes rigid.

"Are you accusing me of something?"

"No, I just find it interesting."

"I don't," Cher says. "I'm pissed the fuck off. I don't care if you were drunk, Eric, you're a grown-ass man and that's not an excuse. Stop acting like a child and get your shit together. Respect your bandmates and their wives already, you dumb-ass man child."

Lori and I stand, slow-clapping in support of Cher's lecture, but Eric scowls.

"I'm single," he insists. "I can fuck whomever I want. And I own part of that bus, so if I want to fuck one or ten women in it, I will."

"Looks like you'll be taking your own fucking bus from now on," Cher replies. "Because I'm not okay with that."

"I'm not either," I add. "I put up with a lot. We all do. But not that. So fuck them all day long and have your dick fall off from all the VD you're gonna get, but don't do it when my husband is on the same bus. It's a douche move."

"It's old news," Leo says. "And it's not typical. Since Lori set the rule years ago, this is the first time it's happened."

"Yeah, and Jake couldn't keep his fucking mouth shut," Eric grumbles.

"That, right there," Cher says, pointing at Eric, "is why I hate touring. Because you say shit like that, and now I can't help but wonder what else happens that we're not privy to. It's not cool, Eric."

"There's nothing that you're not privy to," DJ assures her. "I talk to you every single night."

"They're dumb," Gary says with a sigh. "Nothing happens. I don't even know why Jake said something."

"Because it was funny," Jake says with a shrug. "I didn't think it was a big deal."

Oh, it's a big deal.

We drop the subject, but the rest of the evening is quieter, and everyone leaves earlier than they normally would.

I'm already in our bedroom when Leo walks in after saying goodnight to everyone. They're staying at a hotel downtown.

"Well, that was a shitshow," I say.

"I'm sorry," Leo says, dragging his hand down his face. He looks like sex on a stick, standing in the doorway, with his tattoos and the lip piercing, his hair spikey.

He's my rockstar, my love.

I want to jump him.

I also want to strangle him.

"I should have told you about Eric's fuckery."

"Yes, you should have, but I don't really give a shit about Eric. I know he's a dumbass, and Cher's right, he needs to grow the fuck up."

I don't want to argue in our bedroom, so I stomp past Leo, out to the second floor living space.

"Then what's wrong?"

"Leo." I take a deep breath, then turn to him. "I knew this would turn into a brainstorming session for a new album and tour. I knew it."

"We didn't brainstorm a new album."

"No, you just wrote about six songs and talked about touring non stop." I throw my hands in the air. "I'm not okay with that, Leo. You promised me you'd take a year off."

"And I am," he says. His voice is hard, and his jaw ticks from clenching it. "I just enjoyed a day with my friends."

I prop my hands on my hips and stare at him. I can't win this argument. Ever.

"Sam, you knew that this is what I do when you married me."

"I know that. And I love you. I want to see more of you."

"We have a two-week rule," he insists. "I've never broken that."

"Yeah, they get two weeks, and I get two days. In the six years we've been together, I've never complained. Not once. Because you're right, I did know what I was getting myself into. And I'm damn proud of you. But it's hard, Leo."

"Are you going to ask me to choose, Samantha? Between you or music?"

My whole body breaks out in a cold sweat.

"What if I am?"

His hands ball into fists. "That's not fair."

I turn away from him, marching through the space, looking through tear-filled eyes at this magnificent house he built for me, and how wonderful our life is.

"You know, you gave me this gorgeous home. You've built an amazing life for me." I turn back to him. "And I live it alone. How is that fair?"

He flinches, and I feel like I'm dying inside.

"I miss my husband, and I'm not going to apologize for that, Leo. Don't you miss me when you're gone? Don't you get even a little homesick?"

"Of course! I love you! I'm doing all of this for you."

"Don't you dare put this all on me, Leo Nash. That's not fair either." I point a finger in his chest, watching as his nostrils flare with frustration and anger. "I have everything I could possibly want and more. I just want you. I want a marriage with my husband.

"I'm not asking you to choose. Making music is part of who you are, and I'm so in love with you it makes me stupid. But I need you to give as much time and energy to me as you give to music."

I take his hand and press his palm against my cheek. "You don't have to choose. You can have both."

He frames my face in his hands and tips his forehead against mine, and just this little touch soothes me immediately.

"I'm sorry that you're lonely."

The tears slip down my cheeks now.

"I didn't get married to be alone," I whisper. "I can't do it anymore. I'm not just sharing you with the music. I'm sharing you with the band, and all of the fans. You're not just out on tour, Leo. You're a guest judge on the Voice, and you're making guest appearances somewhere every other week."

"I can back off on a lot of that," he says. "Sam, you're so fucking independent. I know you can do your thing without me."

"Yes, I can, but that doesn't mean that I want to, or that I don't need you, Leo. I need a partnership with you. I'm not just your biggest fan, I'm your wife, and I want to have the chance to prove that I'm good at that."

"You're excellent."

"But how do you know? In six years, I've only had the chance to be with you for a few months, if we add it all together."

"I'm sorry." He crushes me to him, holding me fiercely. "The job is a habit, Sam. It's been a part of my life for so long, it just is. I wish you'd talked to me about this sooner."

"I didn't want you to think that I don't support you. Because you know I do. But I need you."

"You always come first, Sunshine. If you don't want me gone, I won't be gone."

"It's not just about you," I remind him. "You have a band, and they love the work."

"Look, we already promised you a year, and we're going to keep that promise. But I can also promise you this: going forward, we will release an album and tour no more than every other year. We can play it by ear from there."

"You'd do that?"

Why am I surprised? I know him. I should have known that all I had to do was talk to him.

"Anything." He pulls me to him again and buries his face in my neck. "I'd do anything for you, Samantha Nash. I love you, every damn day of my life, and that's never going to change. You want me to give it all up today? Done."

"No." I pull away and shake my head emphatically. "I don't want that. But the every other year thing sounds like a good compromise."

"I think so, too." He kisses my nose and I trace the tattoo on his shoulder. "What am I going to do with all of my free time?"

"Gardening? You could learn to cook. Oh! You could probably work at Nic's bakery."

His lips are twitching with humor as he lays them gently over my own.

"I might take my own advice and write music for other artists."

"That's a great idea."

"Starla called not long ago, asking if I had any new stuff."

"Except for her," I reply, pulling back to glare at him. "No working with women you've boned before."

"Another rule?"

"Hell yes."

He chuckles and bites my earlobe, sending shivers up and down my back.

"Okay, I can live with that rule."

"But I like the idea of you writing music. You could even produce some if you wanted."

His eyebrows rise in thought. "That's not a bad idea. There are studios in Seattle, and I could even work out of the house a bit."

"See? You'll fill your time with plenty."

"I'll be able to make love to you more often."

I bite my lip and groan when he cups my ass and presses against me.

"Yes, that's one hell of a perk."

"Sunshine?"

"Hmm?"

"Every damn day."

"I love you too. Every day."

A ROCKSTAR REUNION

Smoked Chicken Salad

Mushroom Swiss Burger with Garlic Aioli

Chicken Bacon Ranch Kabobs

Grilled Corn 3 Ways

Fried Chicken and Potato Salad

BBQ Ribs with Bacon and
Brown Sugar Baked Beans

Deviled Eggs 3 ways

Lemon Meringue Pie

S'mores Trifle

Smoked Chicken Salad

1 Smoked Chicken

2 cups mayonnaise

¼ cup Dijon mustard

½ cup sweet pickle relish

1 teaspoon salt

1 teaspoon pepper

¼ cup dried cranberries

¼ cup chopped pecans

Remove the bone and skin from the chicken. Place the chicken in a food processor and pulse 2-3 times to break apart large pieces. Add the mayonnaise, Dijon mustard, sweet pickle relish, salt and pepper and pulse again. Transfer the chicken salad to a large bowl and fold in dried cranberries and pecans.

Smoked Chicken

1 whole (5-6 pound) chicken, cut in half

2 tablespoons butter

2 tablespoons Montreal steak seasoning

Vinegar BBQ Sauce (see p. 85)

4 cups hickory wood chips

Gently rub both sides of chicken with butter, including under the skin (best part). Season both sides with Montreal seasoning. Prepare a smoker to smoke at 275 degrees. While the smoker is heating, place the hickory chips in a bowl of water for at least 15 minutes. Once the smoker has reached 275 degrees, add the wood chips and place the chicken on a rack, skin side up. Cover and smoke. The chicken will take approximately 2 hours to reach an internal temperature of 165 degrees. While the chicken is smoking, baste with a generous amount of the vinegar based sauce every 30 minutes (4 times total). Remove the chicken from the smoker and allow to rest for at least 10 minutes before serving.

Quick tip: Vinegar is a natural meat tenderizer. If you do not have the ingredients to make the vinegar-based sauce, simply add ¼ cup white vinegar to 2 cups of your favorite BBQ sauce and stir to combine.

Mushroom Swiss Burgers with Garlic Aioli

Garlic Aioli

1 cup mayonnaise

1 tablespoon minced garlic

1 teaspoon salt

1 teaspoon pepper

3 tablespoons lemon juice

Burgers

1 pound ground beef

1 teaspoon salt

1 teaspoon pepper

1 teaspoon garlic powder

1 teaspoon onion powder

1 teaspoon paprika

1 tablespoon Worstershire sauce

1 tablespoon butter

1 cup baby bella mushrooms, thinly sliced

4 slices Swiss cheese

4 hamburger buns

In a small bowl, combine the mayonnaise, garlic, salt, pepper and lemon juice. Cover and refrigerate for at least 30 minutes. In a large bowl, combine the ground beef, salt, pepper, garlic powder, onion powder, paprika and Worstershire sauce. Form into 4 (¼ pound) burger patties. Heat butter in a large saucepan over medium heat. Place mushrooms in pan and sauté for 3-5 minutes or until they are tender. Remove from heat and set aside until ready to build the burgers. Using a gas grill over high heat, grill the burgers for 3 minutes, then flip and grill for an additional 4-5 minutes or until desired doneness. Place one slice of Swiss cheese on each burger during the last minute of cooking. Remove burgers from the grill. Spread a generous amount of Garlic Aioli on each side of the sesame seed buns. Place the burgers on top of the buns and top with sautéed mushrooms.

2 tablespoons ranch seasoning

2 cups sour cream

¼ cup lemon juice

2 boneless skinless chicken breasts, cut into 1-inch pieces

8 slices bacon, cut in 1/3 pieces

1 red onion, cut into 1-inch pieces

1 red bell pepper, cut into 1-inch pieces

Salt and pepper to taste

6 wooden skewers, soaked in water

In a large bowl, combine ranch seasoning, sour cream and lemon juice. In a large resealable bag, add chicken and half of the ranch marinade. Allow to marinate for 30 minutes. To assemble the kabobs, wrap a slice of bacon around one piece of chicken. Place on the skewer and add one piece of onion and one piece of bell pepper. Continue threading on skewer 3 more times ending with bell pepper. Repeat on the remaining skewers. Baste with half of the remaining marinade. Preheat grill to medium-high heat. Lightly oil the grill grates. Place kabobs on grill and cook for 2 minutes, then turn. Repeat this 5-6 more times until the chicken is cooked through and the vegetables are tender. Serve with remaining ranch marinade.

Grilled Corn 3 ways

8-12 ears of corn in the husk

Mexican Street

Cajun

Pesto and Parmesan

Peel back the husk and remove the silk from each piece of corn, then fold the husk back around the corn. Place the corn in a large pot filled with water and soak for 15 minutes. Remove from water and place on grill over medium heat. Grill for 20-25 minutes, turning halfway through. Remove from grill and peel back the husks. Return corn to grill and cook for an additional 1-2 minutes on each side to add grill marks. Top with any of the 3 toppings below.

Mexican Street

½ cup mayonnaise

½ cup sour cream

1 tablespoon chili powder

3 tablespoons lime juice

1 cup crumbled Cotija cheese

Combine mayonnaise, sour cream, chili powder and lime juice in a small bowl. Spread evenly over corn and top with cheese.

Cajun

8 tablespoons (1 stick) butter, softened

1 tablespoon garlic powder

1 tablespoon onion powder

1 tablespoon paprika

1 tablespoon salt

1 teaspoon pepper

1 teaspoon cayenne pepper

1 teaspoon dried thyme

Combine all ingredients and spread evenly over corn.

Pesto and Parmesan

1 cup basil pesto

1 cup freshly grated Parmesan

Spread pesto evenly over corn and top with grated Parmesan.

Fried Chicken and Potato Salad

2 gallons peanut oil

1 whole (5-6 pound) chicken

2 tablespoons garlic powder

2 tablespoons onion powder

2 tablespoons paprika

2 tablespoons salt

1 tablespoon pepper

1 tablespoon cayenne pepper

In a large stock pot or turkey fryer, heat oil to 365 degrees. Rinse chicken and thoroughly pat dry with paper towels. Combine all seasonings and rub all over the chicken, inside and out. Place chicken in a drain basket or attach to a drop hook. Slowly lower the chicken into the oil. The temperature will drop immediately. Maintain the temperature at 350 degrees for the entire fry time, which is 4 minutes per pound. Remove chicken from oil and drain on paper towels. The internal temperature should be 165 degrees. Allow to rest for 10-15 minutes before slicing.

Potato Salad

5 russet potatoes, peeled

1½ cups mayonnaise

¼ cup Dijon mustard

¼ cup sweet pickle relish

3 hard boiled eggs, chopped

1 tablespoon paprika

1 teaspoon salt

1 teaspoon pepper

In a large pot, add potatoes and fill with water until potatoes are covered. Cover and bring to a boil. Reduce heat to low and cook for an additional 25-30 minutes or until potatoes are tender. Drain and allow to cool enough to handle. Cut potatoes into 1-inch cubes and place in a large bowl. In a separate bowl, combine remaining ingredients and add to potatoes. Toss gently to coat and serve with additional paprika on top.

BBQ Ribs with Bacon and Brown Sugar Baked Beans

1 (2-3 pound) slab baby back ribs

For the rub:

½ cup dark brown sugar

1 tablespoon garlic powder

1 tablespoon onion powder

1 tablespoon paprika

1 tablespoon salt

1 teaspoon pepper

1 teaspoon cayenne pepper

Using a sharp knife, remove silver skin from ribs along the rack. Rinse ribs and thoroughly pat dry. Combine the ingredients for the rub and cover the ribs entirely, being liberal with coverage. Allow to set for 10-15 minutes at room temperature. Heat one side of grill to medium-high heat. Place ribs on opposite side so that the ribs cook over indirect heat. Baste ribs every 10 minutes with Vinegar BBQ Sauce for a total cooking time of 45-55 minutes. Remove ribs from heat and double wrap in aluminum foil. Return to grill on low heat and cook for an additional 20-25 minutes. Remove from grill and allow to rest for 10 minutes before slicing.

Vinegar BBQ Sauce

2 cups white vinegar

½ cup ketchup

¼ cup brown sugar

1 tablespoon salt

1 teaspoon pepper

1 teaspoon garlic powder

1 teaspoon onion powder

In a small pot over low heat, combine all ingredients and bring to a boil. Reduce heat to low and simmer for 10 minutes. Remove from heat, allow to cool and transfer to a Mason jar. Store for up to 2 weeks in the refrigerator. Shake well before each use.

Bacon and Brown Sugar Baked Beans

6 (15.5 ounce) cans pork and beans

8 thick slices bacon, diced

½ cup green onion, chopped

1½ cups Sweet Baby Ray's BBQ sauce

¾ cup dark brown sugar

Preheat oven to 350 degrees. Combine all ingredients in a large bowl and pour into a 9 x 13-inch baking dish. Bake for 90 minutes.

Deviled Eggs 3 ways

Classic Southern

6 hard-boiled eggs

½ cup mayonnaise

1 tablespoon yellow mustard

2 tablespoons Durkee Famous Sauce

2 tablespoons sweet pickle relish

Salt and pepper to taste

Sliced green olives

Paprika

Slice eggs in half and remove yolks. Place yolks in a bowl and smash with a fork until most lumps are removed. Add mayonnaise, mustard, Durkee Famous Sauce, relish, salt and pepper. Mix well and add to egg whites until cups are full. Place one green olive on each egg's filling and sprinkle with paprika. Serve on your favorite deviled egg tray.

Pimento Cheese

1 (4 ounce) jar pimentos, not drained

8 ounces shredded sharp cheddar (yellow)

8 ounces shredded sharp cheddar (white)

1 teaspoon garlic powder

1 cup mayonnaise

6 hard-boiled eggs

Mix all filling ingredients and refrigerate for at least an hour. Slice eggs in half and remove yolks. Place yolks in a resealable bag and refrigerate for another use. Fill each egg white half with pimento cheese and serve.

Chicken Salad

1 rotisserie chicken, shredded

1 cup mayonnaise

2 tablespoons Dijon mustard

¼ cup sweet pickle relish

½ cup chopped celery

¼ cup + 2 tablespoons chopped pecans

1 teaspoon salt

1 teaspoon pepper

6 hard-boiled eggs

Mix all filling ingredients together in large bowl except 2 tablespoons chopped pecans. Slice eggs in half and remove yolks. Place yolks in a resealable bag and refrigerate for another use. Fill each egg white half full of chicken salad and top with pecans.

Lemon Meringue Pie

1 refrigerated pie crust

3 egg yolks

1½ cups sugar

⅓ cup cornstarch

1½ cups water

3 tablespoons butter

½ cup lemon juice

3 egg whites

6 tablespoons sugar

¼ teaspoon vanilla extract

Preheat oven to 400 degrees. Unroll pie crust and press firmly against bottom and side of 9-inch pie plate. Trim overhanging crust from rim of pie plate. Prick bottom and side of pastry thoroughly with fork. Bake 8 to 10 minutes or until light brown; cool on cooling rack. In small bowl, beat egg yolks with fork. In a medium saucepan, mix 1⅓ cups sugar and cornstarch, then gradually stir in water. Cook over medium heat, stirring constantly, until mixture thickens and boils. Boil, stirring constantly for 1 minute. Then, stir half of hot mixture into egg yolks to temper the eggs, then pour back into hot mixture in saucepan. Boil, stirring constantly for 2 minutes; remove from heat. Stir in butter and lemon juice. Pour mixture into pie crust. In a medium bowl, beat egg whites with an electric mixer on high speed until foamy. Beat in sugar 1 tablespoon at a time until stiff and glossy. Mix in vanilla last. Spoon onto hot pie filling and spread, sealing meringue to edge of crust to prevent shrinking. Bake 8 to 12 minutes or until meringue is light brown. Cool for an hour before serving.

For the brownie layer:

8 tablespoons (1 stick) butter, melted

1 cup sugar

2 eggs

1 teaspoon vanilla

⅓ cup cocoa powder

½ cup all-purpose flour

¼ teaspoon baking powder

Preheat oven to 350. Grease an 8 x 8-inch pan. Combine butter, sugar, eggs and vanilla in a large bowl. Add in cocoa powder, flour and baking powder. Pour and spread into greased pan. Bake for 25 minutes.

For the marshmallow layer:

4 ounces cream cheese

4 cups marshmallow cream

1 container whipped topping

In a large bowl, using a hand mixer, combine all ingredients.

To build trifle:

1 box honey flavored Teddy Grahams

1 cup milk chocolate chips

1 cup mini marshmallows

In a trifle bowl, place half of the brownies broken apart in the bottom of the dish. Top with half of the marshmallow layer. Top with 1 cup of Teddy Grahams. Repeat layers again and top with chocolate chips, marshmallows and Teddy Grahams.

Dominic & Alecia

INVITE YOU TO CELEBRATE

CUPPA DI VITA VINYAD'S

RECOGNITION OF

Winery of the Year

IN

WINE MAGAZINE

SATURDAY ~ 7:00 PM

CUPPA DI VITA

RSVP ALECIA BY MONDAY

Dominic and Alecia

Alecia

I'm ready.

I've gone through my list fourteen times. Everything is as perfect as it's going to get.

It's an important night for my husband, and I want it to go off without a hitch.

I march into the kitchen of the vineyard, and my home, where my best friend and caterer extraordinaire, Blake, is working his magic.

"Hey," he says when I walk into the room. "How's it going? You look like Julie the cruise director with that clipboard."

"This is my job, smart ass." I flip him the bird, but Blake just laughs at me. "How's it going in here? It smells amazing."

"Of course it smells amazing. I'm cooking." He points to the stove. "I have the chicken marsala simmering over there. The beef Wellington is in the oven, and the grilled flank steak is ready to go. I have fish tacos, too."

"It's a lot of protein," I mutter, but he just shakes his head.

"I'm the boss of the kitchen, and I know what I'm doing. You have a freaking huge family, Alecia. And they don't all eat the same things."

"You've got me there." I sigh and glance about, satisfied that Blake does in fact have everything under control. "They should be here soon, so I'm doing a final sweep through to make sure everything is good to go."

"I've seen it outside," Blake replies and wipes his hand on the white towel flung over his shoulder. "It looks amazing. I love what you did with the twinkle lights. The food is going to rock, of course."

"Of course."

"And this isn't a party for a bunch of strangers, Leesh. This is your family, and they're going to have an amazing time no matter what."

"You're right." I nod and take a deep breath. "You're totally right. I just want to make it special. Dom deserves it."

"I'd say you've accomplished that. He's going to love it, and you'll have a great time."

The doorbell rings, and the butterflies take up flight in my belly.

"It's show time," I say, take a deep breath, and leave my clipboard in the kitchen, in case I need it later.

"Well hello there, beautiful," Steven Montgomery says when I open the door. He's dressed in a coat and tie, and he wraps me up in a big hug.

"I know we're a little early," Gail says when it's her turn for a hug. "But Steven's excited for tonight."

"I am, too," I assure her. "You're always welcome anytime."

"How are you feeling, dear?" Gail takes my hand and gives it a squeeze. Two months ago, I would have broken down into tears, but I've healed a lot since the miscarriage earlier this year. No one but Gail and Steven knew that I'd been pregnant.

"I'm actually doing much better," I reply honestly. "Thank you for asking."

"Oh, I'm so glad," Gail says with a smile. "Where's Dominic?"

"He's in his office. Feel free to wander out back, or anywhere really, and I'll go find him. We have some bottles of wine open, and there are appetizers out for you as well."

"We'll make ourselves at home," Steven assures me.

I love Dominic's family. I didn't know that I could fit into a group of people as seamlessly as I have this one. They're diverse and funny, and they've welcomed me with open arms.

I wander up the stairs toward Dom's office, and as I approach, I can hear his voice, so I pause outside the door.

"No, I haven't told her."

His voice is hard. I scowl and lean in, wanting to hear more.

"Don't worry, I have this handled. It's about time you got this figured out. It's taken far too long."

What the hell?

"Good. See that you do."

He hangs up and walks out of his office, seeing me in the hallway. His face transforms into a happy smile.

"You have good timing."

"I was just coming to find you," I say. "Your parents just got here."

"They can wait a moment." He pins me against the wall and leans into me.

"Do not mess my hair," I say sternly, but he just laughs. "I mean it, it took me forever to make it look like this."

"You're gorgeous no matter what you do. And I'm not going to get you alone again for a few hours, so I want a moment with you."

When he says things like that, my whole body breaks out in goose bumps. How did I get so lucky that this is my husband?

"Well, how can I say no to that?"

His lips twitch before they land on mine. The kiss starts slow, easy, and then he sinks in and devours my mouth, his hands cupping my shoulders to hold me in place. Not that I plan to go anywhere.

He groans and shifts his stance, sliding one thigh between my legs, and I can't help but rub against him, already throbbing for him.

"We don't have time for this," I murmur against his lips. Dominic is a world-class kisser. I don't know how he does it, but every damn time he kisses me it feels like the first time.

It's almost ridiculous.

"Later then," he whispers, pressing soft kisses to each cheek. "Before we go down there, thank you Tesoro, for everything. You've worked hard for tonight, and it means the world to me."

"You mean the world to me," I reply. "And I wanted this celebration to be special. You've more than earned it."

"You're amazing." He kisses me once more, still full of longing and passion, then takes my hand and leads me down the hallway.

I can hear more voices downstairs.

"I'm quite sure Alecia wouldn't put this out here if we couldn't eat it," Will insists, making me grin.

"Sounds like more of them are here," I say, making both of us laugh.

"Will always sniffs out the food."

"Let's go through the kitchen," I suggest. "You can say hello to Blake before we get sucked into the wonderful black hole that is your family."

"Good idea," he replies, leading me through the back door of the kitchen. Blake glances up and grins.

"Hey, fancy people."

"Thanks for all of this," Dom says. "Are you sure we can't pay you for it?"

"Nah, it's my congratulatory gift. Besides, mentioning me in the magazine article more than tripled my business this month. Trust me, I'm happy to do this."

"We appreciate it," I say, snuggled up to my husband's side. "How's Emily?"

Emily is my former assistant, and Blake's wife. She had a baby just a few months ago.

"She's great. She wanted to come today, but we couldn't find a sitter."

"Oh, she should have come anyway. Everyone's bringing their kiddos tonight," I reply. "You should call her and have her come. There's plenty of room and food, and I'd love to see her and the baby."

Blake grins, then shrugs. "I'll see what she's up to." He turns to Dom. "Did you get everything figured out?"

I frown up at my husband, but he doesn't bat an eye, just nods once.

"Thanks again, Blake."

He leads me out the back door to the back yard, where the family has gathered under the tent and all of the twinkle lights.

"This is beautiful."

"You provide an amazing backdrop." He kisses the crown of my head. I wonder what he was talking about in his office. What hasn't he told me? Was he even talking about me?

And if not, who the hell is her?

Just as Dom predicted, we're both swept up in the sea of our family, chatting and laughing with our guests. Kids zoom past, and babies cry, but are quickly soothed.

Dom's voice was hard on the phone. Like he was angry. It must be bad news.

I bite my lip and nod, as if I'm following Jules and Natalie's conversation.

Are we going to lose the vineyard? Is it a financial problem?

God, I hope not. I love this place as much as if it were a living, breathing member of our family. Besides, that can't be it. He was just featured in Wine Magazine as the winery of the year.

We're definitely not going out of business.

"I want to do a girl's night," Natalie announces just as Samantha and Meredith join us.

"I'm all in, but please don't schedule it for the end of September," Sam says and pops an olive in her mouth. "Because Leo is finally taking me on a proper honeymoon."

"That's awesome," Jules says. "Where are you going?"

"Somewhere tropical," Sam replies with an excited smile. "I'm going to park my ass in a beach chair for two weeks, and no one can stop me."

"Atta girl," Nat says, patting her shoulder. "So, how about next weekend?"

"Can we do the week after?" Meredith asks. "We've finally moved into our new house, and we're doing an open house-style housewarming party next Saturday."

"Fun," Nat replies. "There are so many amazing things happening for the family. I love it. Of course we should do the following weekend. Put it on your calendars. Girl's night, my house, no boys allowed."

"Done," I say, mentally making the note.

I glance across the room, looking for Dom. He's talking with Isaac and Luke, and his gaze turns to mine. He winks, making my stomach clench.

Of course my mind wants to go down the darkest paths possible. I over think every single thing.

Could he be cheating on me? Was he talking to a woman, and she was pressing him to tell me about her? Maybe he's bored with me?

Or maybe it's because I can't seem to get pregnant.

I look his way again, to find him still watching me, and I know that's not it. I know it. A man doesn't kiss me the way he does, or just love me the way he does and then fool around.

Dominic wouldn't do that to me.

Why am I thinking all of these stupid things, anyway? It's probably nothing at all. I need to just ask him later when we're alone.

He'll tell me.

"Right, Alecia?"

I blink rapidly, focusing on Amelia, a cousin of the Montgomerys, and a new client of mine, who I didn't even realize joined us.

"I'm sorry, I didn't hear you. What was that?"

"We're coming along on the wedding plans," she says, watching me closely. "Are you okay?"

"Oh yeah." I wave her off and smile at the group. "I'm totally fine, just running through mental lists for tonight to make sure I didn't forget anything."

"Have you seen this place?" Jules asks. "You clearly didn't forget anything. It's absolutely stunning."

"Thank you."

"Tell us more about Amelia's wedding," Meredith says. "She said it's going to be here at the vineyard?"

"That's right." I'm able to relax while I tell them about our plans. Talking about my job always puts me at ease because I love it and I know it inside out.

"She's not a bridezilla, is she?" Nat asks, bumping Amelia with her hip.

"Not at all," I assure them. "In fact, Lia is quite laid back."

"Whoa," Lia says in surprise. "I think I'm high strung and a basket case."

"Girl, you don't even know what high strung looks like. I once had a bride break down into a full-blown temper tantrum because the wedding cake baker didn't offer chamomile tea as a cake flavor."

"Wait, they have that?" Jules asks, scrunching up her nose.

"I guess she saw it on Pinterest, and decided she had to have it." I shrug. "So no, you're not a problem."

"Anastasia and I are going dress shopping next week," Lia says with a smile. "And she's making the cake, of course. We'll have to ask her about the chamomile tea flavor, although that doesn't sound delicious."

"I'm so happy that we finally have another person in our family getting married," Meredith says with a smile. "It's been a while."

"Mostly everyone's having babies now," Jules says. "How is Hudson, by the way?"

Meredith and Mark have two kids. Lucy is two and Hudson is just a couple months old.

"He's a good eater, that's for sure. He's with Mark somewhere."

Yeah, everyone's having babies. And we will too. Hopefully sooner rather than later because my clock is ticking like crazy.

"Are you going back to dancing, Mer?" Jules asks.

"Well, I'll always have the studio," she replies. "Jax and I will do that until we die. It's fun to teach the kids."

"Our kids all love it," Nat says with a nod.

"And you keep us in business." Mer winks. "Starla called not long ago and asked Jax and me to choreograph her next tour, so we will probably do that."

"So exciting," I say, clapping my hands. "I love her new album."

"Home wrecker," Sam mumbles under her breath and takes a sip of wine, making us all laugh.

"She never tried to wreck your home," Mer says. "Leo and Starla are ancient history."

"I know," Sam says with a smile. "I'm being petty. I'm sure she's nice. She just doesn't get to be around my husband."

"Totally understand," I say, patting Sam's back. "Hey guys, I'm going to go have a word with Dom, and find out how much longer we have until dinner."

I look around and see Dom standing near the edge of the tent talking to his brother, Matt. Their heads are together, and both of them are frowning.

"Hey guys."

They immediately stop talking, and stare at me as if I'm interrupting something important.

"Everything okay?" I ask.

"Of course, what do you need?" Dom asks, and I'm taken aback by his brisk tone.

"Uh, nothing. I just wanted to let you know that I was going to check on dinner."

Dom just nods and I walk away, completely confused.

My God, is Dominic in trouble? Is that what the phone call was about? Is Matt giving him advice?

Holy shit.

I set my thoughts aside, more determined than ever to ask Dom what's going on after everyone goes home.

Blake is just plating the food in the kitchen when I walk in. Servers are hurrying about, getting ready for the busy dinner service.

"Shall I have everyone take their seats?"

"Yep," he says, not looking up. "Perfect timing."

I march back out to the tent, clink a spoon against a water glass to get everyone's attention, and announce, "Dinner is served."

Dominic

Steven, my father, clinks his water glass, catching our attention. We've pretty much finished the main course, and it seems that Blake has another hit on his hands.

Everyone enjoyed their meals.

"I'd like to say something," Steven says as he stands. He's directly across from me, looking about the room with love and kindness, the way he always does when we're all together. "I'm incredibly proud of you, Dominic, and what you've built here at Cuppa di Vita. Not just because of the recognition in the magazine, which is a great honor, but also because you're doing what you love with the woman you adore."

He reaches down for Gail's hand, linking their fingers.

"There's nothing more important than family. If everything else was gone, the ones who love you would still be here. Thank you for letting us celebrate with you today."

He raises his glass, and the rest of us follow suit.

"To Dom and Alecia."

"To Dom and Alecia," everyone repeats.

"Now it's my turn," I say as I stand and button my jacket, looking around at a room of former strangers who now mean more to me than anything. "You're right, the recognition in the magazine is a great honor. It's not just mine, but it also belongs to all of my staff and their families, who sacrifice their time so that the vineyard can be a success.

"I had a vision for this place when I bought it ten years ago. I can't believe it's been that long now."

Everyone nods in agreement.

"And I can honestly say that we've far surpassed any vision that I had back then. I don't think I knew how to dream big enough."

I glance down at Alecia, who's watching me with wide blue eyes.

"And then this amazing woman came into my life, and I knew what it truly meant to dream. To plan. To want more. None of this would be possible without you, Tesoro. You are my muse, you keep my feet firmly planted on the ground, and you support my ambitious ideas. Thank you for being mine. I love you."

"I love you too," she mouths as the family erupts into applause.

I return to my seat and cup Alecia's face in my hands, pressing my lips to hers.

"You didn't have to do that," she says.

"It's absolutely true."

She smiles softly, then gets pulled away by Brynna, who wants to talk about a birthday party for their youngest, Michael.

"I didn't think you'd ever want to leave your house," Nate says to Mark. "You love that place."

"Oh, we're not selling it," Mark insists. "I worked my ass off on that house. We'll rent it out for now. We've just outgrown it. Who knew that two kids and a dog took up so much space?"

"It's not the kids," Isaac says with a laugh. "It's all of their crap."

"True story," Mark replies with a nod. "Isaac had drawn these plans years ago, and put them away. I loved them, and showed them to Mer, and she gave me the thumbs up to build it."

"Congratulations," I say as the servers come around the table, setting chocolate cheesecake in front of all of us.

"Oh, look!" Jules says with excitement. "My favorite."

"Yes, I'm sure they did that just for you," Will says sarcastically.

"Whether they did or didn't, I don't care," Jules says, taking a big bite. "As long as I get two pieces."

"I think Blake made an extra one for you to take home," Alecia says with a wink.

"Hey," Will protests. "What about me?"

"You've eaten enough for six people already," Meg says with a sigh. "You're not even the pregnant woman. That would be me."

"I'll eat for all three of us," Will says with a wink.

"Oh crap, I have to go to the restroom," Meredith says. "Alecia, will you please hold Hudson?"

"Of course."

Mer passes the baby to my wife and hurries inside. Alecia is a natural with babies. She hadn't been around them much until she came into our fold, and she slipped right into an easy rhythm with all of the nieces and nephews, holding and rocking them.

"He's so sweet," she says and kisses his head, then looks up at me. "Isn't he tiny?"

"He looks breakable," I agree, and tuck my finger under his hand, grinning when he grabs on with more strength than I thought he could. "But he's a strong little thing."

Alecia smiles, but there's something in her eyes tonight that I can't put my finger on. She seems distracted, and quieter than usual.

I'll get to the bottom of it later this evening, when we're alone and I can finally give her the surprise I've had up my sleeve for months.

"You're such a little angel," she whispers to the infant, making me smile.

Losing our baby several months ago was gut wrenching for both of us. I know that Alecia will be an amazing mother, and I can't wait to do this with her. To be parents together.

"So what's next, Dom?" Luke asks. "More concerts? Special events?"

"All of those things," I reply with a nod. "I'm having a new amphitheater built on the other side of the property, where it meets the mountain."

"That will be gorgeous," Jules says. "How many will it be able to seat?"

"Five thousand," I reply and offer her my slice of cheesecake.

"You're my favorite brother," she says with a sweet smile and takes a bite of the dessert. "That's going to rock. You should get Nash to open."

"We can only do it if it's next year," Leo says from across the table. "I promised Sam that I won't work this year."

"You could do that," she says, nudging his arm. "It's family."

Leo grins at her. "If you say so, Sunshine."

"That's not a bad idea," I reply, tapping my finger on my lips as I think it over. "It would sell out, that's for sure."

"Think about it. When do you think you'll be ready to open?"

"The timing works well too," I reply. "I won't be ready until next spring."

Leo lifts an eyebrow. "Well, then I'm definitely in. Keep me posted, and we'll work it out."

"Thank you."

Leo raises his glass in cheers and we take a sip. Yes, my family is constantly surprising me. The lengths they'll go to to help each other moves me. I'd known love and closeness before I found them, but it's no less surprising.

The rest of the evening is full of more laughter, children yawning and playing, and Brynn and Caleb's twins with their noses stuck to their phones.

"We should get this little one home," Meredith says, taking a now sleeping Hudson from Alecia. "Thanks for putting him to sleep for me."

"He's just the sweetest thing. It wasn't a problem at all," Alecia replies.

And so begins the mass exodus of the family, making their rounds of saying goodbye and beginning their hour-long journeys home all over Seattle.

"Don't worry," Alecia says to Lia as we walk them out. "It's going to be awesome. I'll come with you dress shopping. We'll take photos for your Instagram, too. You could run a fun contest, asking fans to guess which dress you choose."

"Oh, that's a great idea," Lia says and hugs Alecia close. "Thank you. Really. I know you're not really doing weddings anymore, but Jules said you're the best, and I'm grateful that you said yes."

"It's fun," Alecia says with a wistful smile. "I kind of miss the weddings, and you're giving me a fix. So thank you for asking. Now, don't worry about a thing, and I'll see you in a few days."

Once we've waved everyone off, we both breathe a long sigh of relief.

"I love them," she begins.

"But they're a lot of work," I finish for her, making her laugh and nod as I take her hand and lead her back inside.

"They really are. But I wouldn't have it any other way."

"I'm glad. I'm also incredibly thankful that I have you alone."

She grins, giving me the side-eye. "Is that so?"

"It's quite so," I confirm. "I have something to discuss with you."

She frowns now and looks nervous so I pull her into my arms and hug her close, enjoying the way her body melts against mine.

"What is it?" I whisper in her ear.

"I don't know, I just have a feeling that you're about to drop something on me and I'm nervous."

"Well, I am." I lead her into my office, the excitement building up inside me. I've been waiting for a long time for this. "Sit."

"I can't sit when I'm nervous."

"Please, amore, sit."

She does as I ask and I nod in satisfaction.

"Okay, I'll be right back."

"Just tell me that you want a divorce," she blurts out and I stop cold, staring at her as if, well, as if she just said that.

"Excuse me?"

"I heard you," she says, her eyes welling with tears. "I heard you on the phone, and you said you hadn't told me something, and your voice was hard like it gets when you're angry or super focused on something. Just tell me that you've met someone else who can give you babies and you're moving on because I just can't take this anymore."

She covers her mouth and lets the tears fall from her eyes, watching me with anguish, and all I can do is fall to my knees before her, pull her hands from her mouth, and hold them firmly in mine.

"Number one, you're invited into my office at any time, day or night, and you can listen in on any conversation I have because I don't have any secrets from you. So you don't have to eavesdrop. You clearly didn't hear the whole call.

"Second, if you ever say something like that again, I'll take you over my knee and spank you silly. Divorce and someone else aren't part of my vocabulary. My God, amore, didn't you hear my speech tonight?"

"I did, I just—"

"Stop talking. You are everything in this world that I'll ever need. Just you. And if we're blessed with children, well, that will be amazing and I'll be grateful. But if we aren't, we'll be okay then, too. Do you understand me?"

She nods and wipes her cheek on her sleeve.

"I sounded frustrated on the phone because I was very frustrated. Now, if you'll wait right here for thirty damn seconds, I'll explain everything."

"Okay," she whispers.

"Alecia, don't ever do anything like that again. You know better than that."

She nods and I kiss her lips, then hurry from my office to the spare room where I always hide the gifts I buy her. I have to make a stop at the kitchen where Blake's waiting, unbeknownst to Alecia, with the other part of her present, and I hurry back to my wife.

She's not crying anymore, but her cheeks are stained from the tears.

It always guts me when she cries.

Her eyes are on the two boxes in my hands, both wrapped with silver bows. Her jaw drops.

"What's this? It's not my birthday, or our anniversary."

"You did a lot for me over the past few weeks, and we've had a rough year thus far."

"You're not kidding about that."

"So I decided to do something to cheer us both up."

The bigger of the two boxes starts to wiggle, and a little whimper comes from inside.

"Oh my God," she says, reaching for it. "What's in here?"

"I guess you should open this one first."

She opens the lid and gasps as she pulls out a tiny white, fuzzy puppy that immediately licks her face, his tail wagging like crazy.

"Oh, look at you," she says, crying all over again. "You're so precious. Yes, you are. You're so precious. What's her name?"

"His name will be up to you," I reply. "He's a rescue, so we don't know exactly what kind of pup he is. The vet has some ideas, but we'll have to see as he grows up."

"It doesn't matter," my sweet wife says, kissing the puppy's face. "He's perfect."

"He is pretty cute," I agree, laughing as he spins a circle in Alecia's lap and falls asleep. "That was fast."

"He's a baby," she says, as if that explains everything. "What's in the other box?"

"Open it."

She pulls at the ribbon and rips through the paper.

"Pictures?"

She frowns up at me, and I nod. "Keep going."

"And keys."

She blinks, looking through the photos. "Wait, isn't this that place we stayed at in Hawaii?"

"It is."

"And I said that I loved it so much there that I could live there?"

I nod. I love watching her face as she figures out a riddle.

"What did you do?"

"I bought it for you," I say simply. "I've been working on it for months. That's the conversation that you walked in on. I closed on it today. Now you have a place at the beach where we can escape and relax."

"I don't believe it," she whispers. "My brain was coming up with the most absurd scenarios, and I laughed most of them off, but then I walked up on you and Matt talking, and you acted like I wasn't welcome, and it just made it so much worse."

"I was telling him about the house in Hawaii, and he was asking me where he should take Nic in Italy because he'd like to go there for the holidays before they adopt their newborn. One final trip for just the two of them."

"Oh." She bites her lip and pets the sleeping puppy in her lap. "That's so nice. I'm happy for them."

"I am, too."

She swallows hard. "I'm sorry that I jumped to conclusions."

"You need to always remember that I have our best interests at heart. Both of them. I'm never going anywhere."

"I know that," she says and rolls her eyes. "Trust me, I do. I feel your love every single day. I don't question it. I just overthink and it gets me in trouble."

"Next time, just say, hey babe, what was that about?"

"You make it sound so simple."

"It is." I brush my knuckles down her cheek. "It's truly that simple, amore. There's no need to make it complicated."

"You bought me a house in Hawaii."

"I did."

"When can we go?"

"Whenever you want."

She cups my cheek in her hand and pulls me down for a long kiss.

"As long as we can take little Cabernet here, I'm ready to go tomorrow."

"I like your choice of names."

"I thought you might."

Dinner Party

Chicken Marsala with Homemade Pasta

Seafood Paella

Beef Wellington with Mini Twice Baked Potatoes

Fish Tacos with Citrus Slaw

Smothered Chicken with Mushroom Risotto

Pork Chops with Fig Balsamic Glaze

Grilled Flank Steak with Cheese Grits

Chocolate Cheesecake

Chicken Marsala with Homemade Pasta

4 boneless skinless chicken breasts

Salt and pepper to taste

2 cups flour

¼ cup oil

1 cup button mushrooms, sliced

½ cup Marsala wine

½ cup chicken broth

2 tablespoons butter

Place the chicken breasts 2 at a time in a large resealable bag. Pound with a meat mallet until ¼ inch thick. Season the chicken with salt and pepper, then dredge in flour. In a large skillet, heat oil over medium-high heat. Add 2 chicken breasts that have been dredged in flour to the skillet and fry for 5 minutes on each side. Remove from pan and repeat with remaining 2 chicken breasts. Place chicken breasts on a plate and keep warm. Using the same skillet, reduce heat to low and add the mushrooms and season with salt and pepper. Sauté for 4-5 minutes while lifting the drippings from the bottom of the skillet. Pour in the Marsala wine and let boil for about 30 seconds to cook off the alcohol. Add the chicken broth and simmer for 1 minute. Add the butter and simmer for 1-2 more minutes to allow the sauce to reduce. Place chicken on a bed of Homemade Pasta and pour sauce over the top.

Homemade Pasta

6 cups all-purpose flour

6 whole eggs

1 teaspoon salt (for boiling pasta)

Place the flour on a clean flat surface and make a well in the middle. In a bowl, beat the eggs, then pour into the well of flour. Slowly incorporate the flour into the eggs to begin forming the dough. Continue to knead until the dough comes together and is smooth. Divide dough into 2 portions and wrap with plastic wrap. Allow to rest for 1 hour. Roll out dough on a floured surface until very thin. You should almost be able to see through it. If you have a pasta machine, follow the directions for your desired pasta. If you don't, simply use a pizza cutter and cut strips to the thickness you prefer. Allow to dry on a floured surface for about 5-10 minutes. In a pot of boiling salt water, add the pasta and boil for 2-3 minutes.

¼ cup olive oil

½ cup onion, finely chopped

4 cloves garlic, finely chopped

1 box yellow rice

1 dozen uncooked jumbo shrimp, peeled and deveined

1 bag fresh mussels in shells, cleaned

1 bag fresh clams in shells, cleaned

1 box frozen sweet peas

1 bunch parsley

3 cups chicken broth

1 teaspoon salt

½ cup sliced roasted red bell peppers

In a large paella pan or Dutch oven, heat oil over medium-high heat. Cook onion, garlic and rice with seasoning for 1 to 2 minutes or until onion is soft. Add shrimp, mussels, clams, peas, parsley, chicken broth and salt. Heat to boiling over medium-high heat. Reduce heat to medium-low. Cover and cook for 20 to 25 minutes or until liquid is absorbed, clams and mussels are open, shrimp is pink and rice is cooked. Garnish with roasted peppers.

Beef Wellington with Mini Twice-Baked Potatoes

2 tablespoons butter

¼ pound fresh mushrooms, finely chopped

1 garlic clove, minced

¼ teaspoon dried thyme

1 (17.5-ounce) package frozen puff pastry dough, thawed

4 (4-5 ounce) beef tenderloin steaks, cut 1-inch thick

Salt and pepper to taste

¼ cup Dijon mustard

1 egg

Preheat oven to 425 degrees. In a skillet over medium heat, melt butter and sauté mushrooms, garlic, and thyme 6 to 8 minutes, or until mushrooms are tender. Remove from heat and set aside. Unfold puff pastry sheets and cut each in half crosswise. Spoon mushroom mixture onto center of each of the 4 pieces of puff pastry, distributing evenly. Season both sides of tenderloin steaks with salt and pepper and rub evenly with Dijon mustard. Place steaks over mushroom mixture. Bring corners of pastry up over steaks; using your fingers, pinch corners and edges together to seal completely. Place seam-side down on baking sheet. Whisk together egg and 2 tablespoons of water to make egg wash. Brush evenly over each puff pastry and bake 20 to 25 minutes. Steaks will be medium rare.

Mini Twice-Baked Potatoes

15-20 red potatoes, rinsed and patted dry

1 tablespoon olive oil

1 teaspoon kosher salt

4 tablespoons butter, melted

1 cup sour cream

1 tablespoon mayonnaise

1 cup (plus ½ cup) sharp cheddar cheese

½ cup bacon bits

¼ cup green onion, chopped

½ teaspoon garlic powder

Salt and pepper to taste

Chopped parsley

Preheat oven to 425 degrees. Place potatoes in a large bowl and coat with olive oil and kosher salt. Place on a foil-lined baking sheet and bake for 30-40 minutes or until potatoes are fork tender. Allow to cool for 10 minutes. Cut off the tips of both ends of the potatoes. Using a small spoon or melon baller, scoop out the center of each potato. Place the filling in a large bowl and mash with a fork until smooth. Add butter, sour cream, mayonnaise, 1 cup cheddar cheese, bacon bits, green onion, garlic powder, salt and pepper and stir until combined. Using a small spoon, stuff each of the potatoes with the filling and top with remaining cheddar cheese. Place potatoes on a cookie sheet in a 375-degree oven. Bake for 5 minutes and remove from oven. Garnish with parsley and serve.

Fish Tacos with Citrus Slaw

2 mangos, peeled, seeded and chopped

1 jalapeno, chopped

1 clove garlic, minced

½ Vidalia onion, chopped

1 (8 ounce) can crushed pineapple, drained 1 bunch cilantro, chopped

2 lemons

3 tablespoons oil

1 cup sour cream

4 tablespoons Cajun seasoning

4 grouper fillets

8 taco-size flour tortillas

For the Salsa:

Combine the mango, jalapeno, garlic, onion, crushed pineapple and cilantro in a medium bowl and toss with the juice of one lemon and 1 tablespoon of the oil. Allow to marinate for at least an hour. This can be made a day ahead.

For the Sauce:

Mix together the sour cream, 1 tablespoon Cajun seasoning, and the juice of one lemon. Refrigerate for at least an hour.

Cooking and preparing the Fish Tacos:

Rub fillets with the remaining 3 tablespoons of Cajun seasoning to cover. In a medium skillet, heat 2 tablespoons of oil over medium heat. Place fillets in oil and sear for 2 minutes on each side. Continue cooking in a preheated 400-degree oven for 8-10 minutes depending on the thickness of the fillets. Remove from oven and slice each fillet into 4 pieces. To serve, place 2 pieces of fish in a flour tortilla and top with about 3 tablespoons of salsa and 2 tablespoons of sauce.

Citrus Slaw

1 lemon

¼ cup orange juice

1 tablespoon honey

1 tablespoon Dijon mustard

Salt and pepper to taste

½ cup olive oil

1 bag tri-color slaw

¼ cup cilantro, chopped

¼ cup green onion, chopped

Add juice of one lemon, orange juice, honey, Dijon mustard, and salt and pepper to a blender. Blend on low and slowly add in olive oil until dressing is blended well. In a large bowl, mix together slaw, cilantro and green onion. Pour dressing over slaw and toss to coat. Allow to marinate for 30 minutes and serve.

1 cup mushrooms, sliced
1 onion, thinly sliced
2 tablespoons butter
2 tablespoons soy sauce
6 slices bacon
4-6 boneless, skinless chicken breasts
¼ cup chicken broth
½ cup Honey Mustard Dressing
1 cup cheddar cheese, shredded
4-6 slices provolone cheese

In a large skillet over medium heat, sauté mushrooms and onions with butter and soy sauce until tender, about 5-8 minutes. Remove from skillet and set aside. Fry chopped bacon in the skillet and set aside. In the same skillet, add chicken breasts and sear on each side in bacon grease for 2-3 minutes. In a 9 x 13-inch casserole, pour chicken broth to cover the bottom. Place chicken evenly in dish and cover with Honey Mustard Dressing. Top with mushrooms, onion and bacon, then finally with cheddar and provolone cheese. Cover with foil. Bake at 350 degrees for 30 minutes, then uncover and bake for an additional 15-20 minutes or until chicken reaches 165-170 degrees.

Honey Mustard Dressing

1 cup mayonnaise
½ cup Dijon mustard
½ cup honey
1 tablespoon smoked paprika

Mix all ingredients and store covered in refrigerator for at least an hour before serving.

Mushroom Risotto

2 tablespoons butter

2 cups sliced mushrooms

½ cup diced Vidalia onion

2 cups of Arborio Rice

½ cup white wine

7 cups chicken broth

½ cup green onion, chopped

½ cup grated Parmesan cheese

Salt and pepper to taste

In a medium saucepan over medium heat, melt one tablespoon of butter and add the mushrooms. Cook until soft, about 5 minutes. Remove the mushrooms and set aside for later. Add the other tablespoon of butter to the same saucepan over low heat and cook the Vidalia onion until tender, about 3 minutes. Add rice, stirring constantly for 2 minutes, then pour in wine and stir for an additional 2 minutes. Add 1 cup of broth to the rice and stir until absorbed. Continue this process until all the broth has been added and the rice is al dente. This will be anywhere from 25-30 minutes. Never quit stirring. That's the most important part. Remove rice from heat and stir in the mushrooms, green onion and Parmesan. Add salt and pepper to taste and serve.

2 tablespoons oil

4 bone-in pork chops (1 inch thick)

1 teaspoon salt

1 teaspoon pepper

1 cup chicken broth

¼ cup balsamic vinegar

½ cup Fig Jam (see p. 164)

1 tablespoon fresh thyme, chopped

1 tablespoon butter

Preheat oven to 300 degrees. In a large iron (or oven safe) skillet over high heat, add the oil to coat the bottom. Season the pork chops with salt and pepper and place in the skillet. Sear for 2 minutes on each side. Bake in the oven for 10-12 minutes or until the internal temperature is 145 degrees. Remove from oven and allow to rest on a plate for 10 minutes. While the pork chops are resting, using the same iron skillet over medium heat, add the chicken broth and balsamic vinegar. Cook for 1 minute, scraping the pan with a spoon to remove the delicious bits on the bottom. Stir in the fig jam and thyme and continue to cook for 1-2 minutes. Add in butter and stir to melt. Pour over pork chops and serve.

Grilled Flank Steak with Cheese Grits

¼ cup olive oil

2 tablespoons minced garlic

2 tablespoons red wine vinegar

¼ cup soy sauce

¼ cup honey

1 teaspoon pepper

1 pound flank steak

Combine all of the ingredients except the steak in a large resealable bag. Add the steak and toss to coat. Refrigerate for at least 2 hours to overnight to marinate. Prepare your grill for indirect heat. Make one side high heat and the other side low heat. Remove the steak from the marinade and place directly over high heat. Sear on each side for 2 minutes, then move to low heat and continue cooking until internal temperature is 115 degrees (for medium rare). Remove from the grill and tent with foil to rest for 15 minutes. The steak will continue to cook and the temperature will rise. Slice across the grain to serve.

Cheese Grits

6 cups water

1 tablespoon salt

2 cups milk

4 cups of instant grits

8 tablespoons (1 stick) butter

1 (8 ounce) package cream cheese

2 cups freshly grated Parmesan

2 cups sharp cheddar cheese, shredded

Salt and pepper to taste

The most important step in this recipe is to salt your water first. If you do not, the grits will never be salty enough. Bring the water and milk to a roaring boil and add salt. Boil for 2 minutes then add grits and stir continuously until they begin to thicken. Cover pot and reduce heat to low. Cook for about 5-10 minutes, then remove from heat and add butter and cream cheese. When they have been mixed in well, add the Parmesan cheese and 1 cup of the cheddar cheese. Salt and pepper to taste, then pour mixture into a casserole dish and top with remaining 1 cup of cheddar cheese. Bake at 350 degrees for 30 minutes or until bubbly.

Chocolate Cheesecake

1 package Oreo cookies

6 tablespoons butter, melted

½ cup milk

2 cups semisweet chocolate

3 (8 ounce) packages cream cheese

1 cup sugar

2 eggs

1 teaspoon vanilla extract

2 tablespoons flour

Preheat the oven to 375 degrees. Grease a 9" springform pan with non-stick cooking spray. To make the crust: Crush the Oreo cookies using a food processor. If desired, set aside about a tablespoon of the crumbs to garnish the finished cake. Add the melted butter, processing briefly or stirring until the mixture is evenly crumbly. Press the moist crumbs into the bottom and partway up the sides of the prepared pan. Bake the crust for 15 minutes. Remove from the oven, and set aside to make the filling. Reduce the oven heat to 350 degrees. In a small microwavable bowl, combine the milk and the chocolate chips. Heat in the microwave, stirring frequently, until the chips melt and the mixture is smooth, about 2 minutes, then set aside. In a large mixing bowl, beat together the cream cheese and sugar at low speed with a hand mixer, until thoroughly combined. Add the eggs one at a time, beating to combine after each one. Stir in the vanilla, then the flour. Add the chocolate mixture, beating slowly until thoroughly combined. Pour the batter on top of the Oreo crust in the pan. Bake for 45 to 50 minutes, until a toothpick inserted in the cake comes out clean. Allow the cake to cool for 1 hour. When it's completely cool, cover the cake, and refrigerate it until ready to serve. Garnish the cake with the reserved crumbs.

HOME
sweet
HOME

Help us celebrate
our new home!

Saturday, 2:00-5:00
Drop In
Mark and Meredith's house

Mark & Meredith

Meredith

Fuuuuuuck.

I can't say it out loud. I want to, but my two-year-old, Lucy, is clinging to my leg and repeats everything I say as if it's her damn job.

"Stop worrying," Mark says as he sidles up behind me and wraps his arms around my middle, kissing my neck. "It's going to be awesome."

"I don't have dessert," I say in a panic. "Mark, why didn't I remember the freaking dessert?"

"Because you just finished moving into a new house, have a newborn and a toddler, and run a business?" he suggests. That cocky grin of his lets him get away with a lot.

A lot.

"Mama, hungry," Lucy says while staring up at me with big blue eyes. She has her father's eyes.

"I know, baby. I'm just going to finish putting the bacon cups in the oven and then I'll get you a snack."

She leans her sweet, blonde head against my leg, still clinging. Lucy is sweet, down to her core. She's quiet, and honestly isn't that demanding. She's been that way since the moment she came out of my body on a cold winter day two years ago.

Hudson, however, is always happy to remind us all that he's here, and he wants everything now.

And he's only three months old.

"I've got this," Mark says, picking Lucy up and kissing her chubby cheek before putting her in her booster seat at the table and reaching for her snacks.

"I don't know what I'm going to do," I mutter as I shove the cupcake pan in the oven upside down so the bacon can cook around the cups. "I can't have people come and go throughout the day without serving them dessert."

"I don't understand the point of a housewarming party," Mark says with a shrug as he pops a piece of tomato in his mouth. "I mean, we don't need anything. We're still trying to figure out what to do with half of our wedding gifts from years ago as it is."

"It's not about the gifts. I want to show the new house to our families and friends, and doing it all in one day is the easiest. I already told everyone not to bring anything."

"Like they ever listen to that," he replies. "You've met them. Giving gifts is like breathing."

"Oh, God, I hope they don't bring anything."

"Stop stressing out about all of this," he says and kisses me again, soothing me the way he's done since we were teenagers. "The house looks great, the food's going to be great, and if they want dessert, they can go to Nic's after this. In fact, why don't you just send me over there and I'll buy five dozen or so. That should tide Will over."

"She's busy, and I'm not going to inconvenience her with this short notice." I chew my lip just as Mark's phone rings.

"This is my brother," he says. "Hey, bro. What's up? Yeah, you guys can come over anytime. Sounds good."

"Let me talk to Natalie," I say, hope springing in my chest.

"Hey, Mer wants to talk to Nat. Is she nearby? Great. See you in a bit."

He passes the phone to me. There's shuffling in the background, and then Natalie's soothing voice comes over the phone.

"Hey, Mer. How's it going over there?"

"I'm having a crisis, and I need your input."

"Always happy to help in a crisis," she says with a chuckle. "Tell me."

"I don't know how I did it, but I forgot all about serving dessert today. I don't want to bug Nic. Do you have any ideas?"

"Actually, yes. Jules and I made a ton of these chocolate covered peanut butter truffles yesterday. They're made with Nutter Butters and should be illegal in every state. I'll bring those."

"Oh my God, those sound amazing."

"You'll gain five pounds just from looking at them," she assures me. "And Luke and I went to Montana last month, and I brought back a ton of huckleberries to put in the freezer. I'll call Jenna in Cunningham Falls and ask her for a quick recipe."

"I haven't tried huckleberries yet, so that sounds fantastic. Thanks, Nat. I owe you."

"Trust me, eating all the calories today will be payment enough. I'll call Jenna, and hit the store for ingredients on the way to your place. Luke called to ask if we could come over early and let the kids play outside for the day."

"Of course, you're always welcome here. You know that. Mark built that play yard for the whole family, since we all seem to breed like we're solely responsible for populating the earth."

Nat snorts and assures me they'll be here soon. We hang up and I take a big breath, letting it out slowly.

"Okay, this is handled. Nat's taking care of dessert, and they're coming early so she and I can get it ready."

"See? It's working out," Mark says as he takes Hudson out of his bouncy seat and cuddles him in the crook of his arm. "Now that these two have had a snack, I'll take them up to change their clothes."

"You're the best husband in the history of husbands."

"I know." He flashes that cocky smile and takes the kids upstairs to get ready for the party. I finish with the BLT cups, the hot crab dip, artichoke dip and bruschetta, so when Natalie arrives, we can focus on the dessert.

Natalie is true to her word. Less than thirty minutes later, Luke, Nat, and their whole brood of four kids come bustling into the house. Luke and Mark immediately take the kids outside, and Natalie and I get to work.

"God, I love your backyard," Nat says as she stares outside, holding a cup from Starbucks. "We might be over here all the time from now on."

I stand next to her, taking in our husbands laughing and playing with our kids. Mark is carrying Hudson in a carrier on his front.

"I always melt when we watch them with the kids."

"It's hot to watch handsome guys be good dads," she agrees. "Okay, enough ogling. We have work to do. Jenna gave me the recipe for something called huckleberry delight that sounds, well, delightful."

"I love anything delightful," I reply with a laugh and we dig in.

"Mom, Aunt Mer!" Olivia yells, barreling through the back door. "Stella's here!"

"Let them in," I say to my niece as I measure out the sugar. "Thanks, honey."

"I brought balls," Jules announces, carrying a bag and holding it high, making us giggle. "Thank God you saved me from eating them all myself."

"Nat brought some, too. You made a million of them."

"I was PMSing," Jules says with a shrug. "I was convinced that I wanted to eat all of them. What can I do?"

"Stir these berries," Nat says, passing the spoon. "We're cooking them down and making them thick."

"Can I just eat these with a spoon?" Jules asks.

"I agree," I say. "They smell so good."

"We need to take everyone to the Montana house," Nat says with a smile. "It's awesome there. Maybe this fall we can all go."

"I'm in," I say immediately. "We could use the time away."

"Are you okay, honey?" Jules asks me.

"Oh yeah. I'm just stressed out. Whoever said having two kids is the same as having one was a dirty liar."

"I'm not having any more," Jules says, shaking her head. "This one can pump out a dozen, but one is enough for me."

"We're done at four," Nat says with a grin. "And you're right. Having two is a ton more work than one. But more than that and it's really not so bad."

"I'm finished," I say, shaking my head. "I'm happy with the two we have."

"They're pretty adorable," Jules admits after Nat takes the cooked berries and covers the desserts in the pans, then sets them in the fridge.

"These just need to set up for a bit. In the meantime, I want a tour."

"Me, too," Jules says.

"This is my favorite part of today." I do a little shimmy in the kitchen, then gesture for them to follow me.

And for the next several hours, I give tours of our new home to our friends and family. I can't even begin to describe how proud I am of Mark and Isaac and the whole team who brought this house to life.

"I didn't think I'd ever want to leave our other house," I confide in Sam and Leo later when we're standing in the master bathroom. "I loved it there. But with the kids, we just needed more space."

"Well, you got it," Sam says. "And I love the rustic farmhouse style, with the exposed beams and reclaimed wood."

"I do, too." I grin. "I might have driven Mark nuts with all of my Pinterest boards and constant texts to show him photos of ideas that I liked. But I think it paid off."

"It's beautiful," Leo says with a smile. "Now, I think I'll go outside with the guys and the kids."

"That's the other part I love," I say as I walk with them down the stairs. "Mark built that house that's a tiny replica of this one, along with the jungle gym and swings for the kids, and I think it's perfect for get-togethers like these."

"It definitely keeps them all busy," Sam says with a laugh.

We step outside to find utter chaos.

Wonderful chaos.

Children are scrambling about, laughing and chasing our golden retriever, Lady, and Dom and Alecia's new puppy, Cabernet.

"These BLT cups are just delicious," Gail Montgomery says as she takes another bite of one. "So clever and perfect for a party like this."

"Thank you. They're a favorite around here."

"Aunt Meredith," Stella says, "We want to go see Lucy's room."

Stella's standing with Sophie, Olivia and Lucy, along with their cousins, Michael and Liam.

"Okay, but no food in the house, okay?"

"Okay!"

"They probably want to get out of the heat for a bit," Nat says, fanning her neck. "And I can't say that I blame them."

"It's been a hot summer," I agree. We're sitting under the covered patio, out of the sunshine, and it's still warm. "I'll turn the fans on."

"I need to install fans on my patio," Sam says, looking up at them. "What a great idea."

"I read a thing somewhere that the fans help keep flying bugs away because they don't like the breeze."

"Even better," Sam says.

"Please save me from surly teenagers," Brynna pleads as she plops down next to me and wipes her brow in exhaustion.

"They're not thirteen yet," I reply with a laugh.

"Well, they act like they're thirty," she says with a scowl. "They're both grounded from their phones for the weekend, and you'd think I just cut both their arms off."

"What did they do?" Jules asks.

"They switched places in class so Josie would pass her math test. She struggles with math, but Maddie loves it."

"I wish I'd had an identical twin to help me with math in school," I mutter, earning a glare from Brynna. "Not that it's the right thing to do."

"I know that Mad thought she was helping," Brynna admits with a sigh. "And it's kind of funny, really, but I can't let this slide. If I do, they'll do this all the time, and that's not okay. Josie has to earn her own grades."

"Agreed," I say. "But it sucks when they're mad at you."

"Basically, I think this is just how it's going to be until they graduate from college." Brynna shrugs and takes a bite of the artichoke dip, then sighs. "Thank God for food therapy."

"I'm with you there," Jules says and takes a bite of a BLT cup.

"Um, Aunt Meredith?"

I glance over to see Olivia standing at the patio, her eyes wide. She's biting her lip, and looks nervous.

"Yes, sweetheart?"

"Um, I think I need to show you something."

"Is everything okay?" I ask as I jump out of my seat and hurry after Olivia, who's hurrying through the house and up to Lucy's room.

"We didn't mean to."

Those words never started a fun conversation.

"Mean to what?"

I stop cold when I get to Lucy's room. Stella's holding one of my new white towels, scrubbing my brand-new carpet with it.

One of the pans of huckleberry delight is sitting empty on the floor a few feet away.

And there, in the middle of the floor, is a three-foot by three-foot purple circle of berries and whipped dessert and graham cracker crust.

"What happened?"

They all start to talk at once. Lucy's latched on to my leg, like she always does, and is crying.

I can't understand a thing anyone is saying, so I take a deep breath and say, "Stop talking. Olivia, what happened?"

"We wanted dessert."

"And I told you no food inside."

"I know, but we were going to be careful, and we weren't ready to go outside again," Stella says, her blue eyes filling with tears. "But the boys were fighting over the pan, and it got dropped, and it all fell out. I tried to clean it up."

"All of you, with me. Now." I spin at Nate's voice. I hadn't heard him follow me up. "I'll take care of the kids."

"Thank you."

"Lucy," Nate says, holding his hands out to her. "Let's go downstairs, sweetheart."

Nate's a kind man. Intimidating as all get out, but kind.

He takes the kids downstairs, and I can only lean against the doorjamb and take in the mess.

Brand-new carpet, with huckleberry stains.

"Have kids, they said," I mutter. "It'll be fun, they said. They are dirty liars."

"Who's lying to you?"

I don't turn at his voice. I heard him coming up the stairs. I'd recognize my husband's footsteps anywhere.

"Everyone who said having kids would be fun. Look." I point to the stain and he flinches. "Yeah. Less than a month of being settled in and I already have to replace the carpet."

"To be fair, I suggested hardwood in here."

I glare at him. "Really?"

"Okay, bad timing." He holds his hands up in surrender. "Go downstairs, M. I've got this."

"We can leave it for now. I'll shut the door and we can take care of it later. We have guests. I refuse to ignore them."

"You don't worry about this. I'll handle it."

I sigh again and lean into him when he holds his arms out wide.

"It's been a hell of a day."

"Go enjoy the family," he says, his lips in my hair. "Don't worry."

I stare up at him, press my lips to his, and then nod.

"Let me know if you need my help," I offer.

Mark

"Isaac." I gesture to my friend and business partner, someone I've come to think of as family. "I need your input."

"What's up?" he asks. He's been chatting with Will and Caleb, and all three turn their attention to me.

"There's been an incident."

Three pairs of eyebrows raise.

"Follow me."

We climb the stairs to Lucy's room and I open the door.

"Shit," Will mutters. "What happened in here?"

"It looks like someone wrestled in grape Jell-O."

"Close," I reply, shaking my head. "The kids brought a pan of dessert up here and it ended up all over the floor."

Isaac spies the discarded towel. "And someone tried to clean it up with a white towel?"

"Seems so," I confirm. "So my question is, how do I clean it?"

"Scrap it," Caleb says. "Get new carpet."

"It's brand new," I reply grimly. "Mer loves this carpet."

"You can steam clean it, but it's still going to stain," Isaac says. "But you could put a nice area rug over it."

"I thought of that," I say with a nod. "That might be the way we go for now. I wanted hardwood, but Mer wanted carpet in the bedrooms."

"And our girls get whatever they want," Will adds with a grin.

"Damn right." Caleb nods, surveying the mess. "And I'm assuming Meredith has seen this?"

"She might have been on the verge of a panic attack," I confirm. "I told her to go enjoy her day and I'll worry about it."

"Where do you keep rags that you don't care about ruining?" Isaac asks.

"In the garage."

"You get those and we'll clean this up. I'll go get our steam cleaner, and see what kind of magic we can work here."

"We have an industrial steam cleaner," Caleb offers. "With lots of kids and a dog, it gets used a lot. Plus, I live closer. You guys get started on this and I'll be back."

"He just doesn't want to do the dirty work," Will grumbles after Caleb has left.

"I can't say I blame him," I reply with a laugh. "Let's get this cleaned up."

It takes two hours, two dozen rags, and six passes with the steam cleaner, but by the end of it, most of the stain is gone.

"It'll never look new again," Isaac says with a shrug. "But it's not too bad."

"We can at least live in here until Mer decides what she wants to do with it," I reply. "Thanks for your help, guys."

"Dad! Dad!"

Liam comes running up the stairs, his eyes full of panic. Isaac cups his son's shoulders and bends down on his level.

"What's wrong?"

"Josie fell," the boy says, his chest heaving. Caleb immediately sprints down the stairs to get to his daughter. "She was balancing on the roof of the playhouse, and she lost her balance and fell. She says her leg hurts."

"Shit." We all race downstairs, the stain in the carpet quickly forgotten, to get to the young girl.

By the time we burst into the back yard, Caleb has a crying Josie in his arms, wiping her tears.

"Where does it hurt, jellybean?" he asks.

"My ankle," she cries. "Dad, if it's broken, I won't be able to dance. I have to dance."

"It's okay," he croons as Meg, the nurse of the family, checks Josie out.

"Jose, I'm going to ask you to try to stand on it, okay?" Meg asks. Josie shakes her head no, but Meg takes her face in her hands so Josie listens. "We have to see if it hurts too badly to walk on it so we know if it's broken. It might just be badly bruised."

"Okay," Josie whispers and with Caleb's help, she stands on her good foot, then gingerly tries to take a step. She doesn't crumple to the ground. "It's not too bad."

"I don't think it's broken," Meg says to Brynna as she sits back on her haunches. "But you'll want to take her to the ER, just in case. Get an X-ray."

"Let's go, guys."

"Oh, man," Michael, their youngest, says. "I was having fun with Liam."

"He can stay," Stacy offers with a smile. "The boys can play together. I'll bring him home later."

"Thanks, Stace," Brynna says to her cousin, kisses her cheek, and then Brynna, Caleb and the girls are out the door to the ER, after promising to let us know what the X-ray shows.

"Never a dull moment around here," Meredith says with a sigh. She's holding our sleeping son to her chest while Lucy plays with Olivia and Stella. It never fails to steal the breath from my chest when I see my wife holding one of our babies. This life with her is a dream come true.

A dream that I was never brave enough to think of for too long before she and I rediscovered each other a few years ago.

She's everything I've ever wanted in my life, and the fact that she's mine, along with these amazing kids, is a blessing that I'm sure I don't deserve, but I'll never question.

I don't know what I would do without her.

"Why are you watching me like that?" she asks softly.

"Like what?"

"All mushy like," she says with a laugh.

"I'm pretty mushy whenever I'm around you, M." I press a kiss to her cheek, near her ear. "Because I'm so fucking in love with you."

"I'm sorry I'm late!"

Jax, Meredith's best friend, rushes out the back door, a frown on his face. "I tried to get here earlier, but I ran out of gas. I mean, how does that happen to a man over thirty?"

"You said you put gas in the car," Logan, Jax's husband, grumbles as he follows him outside and heads straight for Mer and the baby. "I'm sorry. It's Jax's fault. Now, let me at that baby."

With a chuckle, Meredith passes Hudson to Logan while Jax marches back inside.

"I'm getting food," he announces.

"He's been an ass today," Logan says, settling in a chair with Hudson on his shoulder. "Seriously, did you fire him or something?"

"I can't fire a partner," Mer says with a laugh. "I'll go talk to him."

She saunters into the house, and I can't take my eyes off of her.

"I hope Isaac still looks at me like that," Stacy says, catching my attention.

"Like what?"

"Like he can't wait to get his hands on me."

"He does," Isaac replies as he joins us. He pulls his wife out of her chair, then sits and tugs her into his lap. "I can't wait to get my hands on you."

"Good answer," she says with a laugh.

"I just got a text from Brynna," Meg announces. "Josie's ankle is not broken."

"Thank God," I say.

"What happened to Josie?" Logan asks.

"She fell and hurt her ankle," I reply. "But it sounds like she's okay."

Jax and Meredith return, with Jax carrying a loaded plate.

"Did you bring me some?" Logan asks.

"No," Jax replies with a frown. "I don't like you right now."

"Nah, you love me," Logan says confidently and reaches over to steal some of Jax's food. "What would you do without me?"

"I wouldn't have run out of gas today," Jax mutters.

"You said you got gas," Logan repeats, making the rest of us snicker.

"Well, when you got in the car and saw the gas gauge was on E, that was probably an indication that I didn't."

"I didn't check it," Logan replies calmly. "And we'll discuss this later."

"Ah, marital bliss," Meredith says with a happy smile. "I'm glad you don't take any of Jax's crap, Logan."

"I don't give anyone crap," Jax says, looking offended.

The rest of the afternoon passes without another incident of injury or destruction. The kids are exhausted, and go down easily after their baths.

It feels like I haven't been alone with my wife for days when we finally collapse on the couch next to each other, staring straight ahead in an exhausted stupor.

"So, today was an adventure," I begin.

"It was a shitshow," she says with a sigh and rubs her hands over her face.

"No, it wasn't."

"How can you say that?" She stares at me with wide eyes. Her hair is a mess. Her makeup is smudged.

And I've never seen anything as beautiful in my life.

"Josie is hurt, our carpet is ruined and I forgot dessert. I never forget stuff like that."

"Mer, cut yourself a break." I wrap my arm around her shoulders and tug her against me. "It's been a busy few months."

"Few years," she mutters and I nod in agreement.

"Exactly. Josie's fine, the carpet can be replaced, and you figured the dessert out. Everyone had a great time, and they got to see our new digs, which is exactly what our goal was. We have a huge family. Things are going to happen."

"I know. I guess I'm still getting used to it," she admits. "I mean, I thought I was used to being a part of the family, and there are many days that I am. I love them all, you know that."

"I know."

"But for a lot of years it was just me and Mom, and Jax. Now that Mom's gone, there are still days that I feel lost, even though your family has been amazing about making me feel welcome and a part of them."

"You are part of them," I reply. "Is Jax okay? What did he say when you went in the house to talk to him?"

"He and Logan have been fighting." She shrugs. "They're going to be fine, but I think they've been wearing on each other's nerves."

"When do you two go to LA to work with Starla?" I ask.

"I don't have to go," she begins, but I press my finger to her lips, hushing her.

"Yes, you do."

"I don't want to leave you and the kids."

"We're going to be great. You'll only be gone for a week. As you know, I have an army of women at my disposal if I need help, which I won't because I'm the dad of the year."

"You really are," she says with a soft smile. "You're the best daddy, M."

"See? I got this. When do you go?"

"In two weeks," she says. "Maybe it'll be good for Jax to get away for a few days."

She sighs, leaning into me even harder. "I've been in a funk this week."

"I know," I say, kissing her head. "It's okay."

"I miss my parents and Tiff," she says softly. "They would love this house. And they would love being with the rest of the family."

She swallows hard. I hate that my wife has been through so much pain in her life. I wish I could wipe it all away. I wish that she was still surrounded by her family.

"Yes, they would," I reply.

"I can picture it, you know?" She swallows again. "Tiff with a husband and little ones, and my parents so proud of us, chatting with your parents and the others. I hate that we were all robbed of that."

"I hate it too."

"Do you think they know?" She pushes away so she can look up hopefully into my eyes. "Do you think they know how happy I am? That they can see us and our kids?"

"I do," I reply with a soft smile and wipe the tears from under her eyes. "And they're so fucking proud of you, M."

She gives me a watery smile and leans into me again. "Yeah. I think so, too. I guess I just get melancholy when good things are happening for us. I feel almost guilty because things are so good, and they will never have that."

"They did have it," I remind her. "Your parents were very happy, and they loved you girls. Your mom told me that a lot back in the day. And Mer? They'd be pissed as all get out if they knew that you felt guilty for being happy. They would want you to be happy."

"I know." She nods and wipes at a tear on her cheek. "And I am happy. Ridiculously happy. I'll pull out of this funk, just like I always do. It helps that I can talk to you about it."

"Always." I kiss her head again, never able to get enough of the smell of her, of the feel of her against me. "You've had a lot to deal with lately, and you're still healing from having Hudson."

"Who might have been the biggest baby ever birthed," she mutters with a sigh. "I'm a small woman, M, and he was almost eleven pounds."

"I remember," I say with a cringe. "I don't know how you did it."

"With a lot of pain," she says with a laugh. "But I'm feeling better. Dancing feels good."

"I'm glad."

She tips her face up for a kiss, and I happily comply, sinking into her soft mouth.

"Never forget," I whisper against her lips. "It's you and me. M and M, against the world."

She grins and cradles my face in her hands. "Always."

House Warming Party

HOT CRAB DIP WITH BREAD RING

BLT CUPS

SPINACH ARTICHOKE ROLLS

STRAWBERRY AND BACON BRUSCHETTA

CHOCOLATE AND PEANUT BUTTER TRUFFLES

From
Kristen's Kitchen...

HUCKLEBERRY DELIGHT

1 (8 ounce) package cream cheese, softened

¼ cup mayonnaise

1 tablespoon minced garlic

Juice of 1 lemon

1 teaspoon onion powder

1 pound lump crab meat

1 cup shredded mozzarella

½ cup freshly grated Parmesan

3 tablespoons chopped fresh parsley

1 teaspoon salt

1 teaspoon pepper

1 tube refrigerated French loaf bread dough

4 tablespoons butter, melted

1 teaspoon garlic powder

Preheat oven to 350° and spray a 9" iron skillet with non-stick cooking spray. In a large bowl, combine cream cheese, mayonnaise, garlic, lemon juice, and onion powder and stir until cream cheese is very smooth. Fold in crab meat, mozzarella, Parmesan, 2 tablespoons parsley, and season with salt and pepper. Cut bread dough into 16 pieces and roll each piece into a small ball. Place bread balls around the perimeter of the skillet, then brush with butter and sprinkle garlic powder on top. Add the crab mixture to the center of the dough ring. Bake until the bread is golden and cooked through and the cheese is bubbly, about 25 minutes. Serve warm.

BLT Cups

12 strips bacon (6 whole strips, 6 cut in half)

1 cup cherry tomatoes, sliced in half

2 cups iceberg lettuce, thinly sliced

1 tablespoon mayonnaise

½ cup sour cream

Juice of ½ lemon

Salt and pepper to taste

Preheat oven to 400 degrees. Using a 6-cup muffin tin, turn the tin upside down and place 2 half-strips of bacon on top, making an X. Then place 1 whole strip of bacon around the sides to form a cup. Repeat with remaining bacon strips. Place muffin tin on a rimmed cookie sheet. Bake for 20 minutes, remove bacon cups from cupcake tin and drain on paper towels. While bacon is cooking, mix together remaining ingredients and scoop into bacon cups when they're done.

Spinach Artichoke Rolls

6 cups oil for frying

1 package frozen spinach, thawed and drained

1 can baby artichokes, chopped

1 (8 ounce) package cream cheese

¼ cup sour cream

¼ cup mayonnaise

½ cup grated Parmesan

1 teaspoon garlic powder

1 teaspoon salt

1 teaspoon pepper

1 package egg roll wrappers

Heat oil to 350 degrees in a Dutch oven or deep fryer. In a large bowl, combine all the ingredients except egg roll wrappers. Place 2-3 tablespoons of filling in the center of each egg roll wrapper. Fold in the two sides, then roll up starting with open corner. Seal with water at the end of the roll. Fry 2-3 minutes. Drain on paper towels and serve.

1 cup ricotta cheese

¼ cup basil pesto

1 French baguette, sliced

2 cups strawberries, sliced

8 strips bacon, cooked and crumbled

1 cup goat cheese, crumbled

Balsamic Glaze

In a small bowl, combine the ricotta cheese and basil pesto. Spread over sliced baguettes. In a separate bowl, combine the strawberries, bacon and goat cheese. Place 1-2 tablespoons on top of each baguette. Drizzle Balsamic Glaze on top.

Balsamic Glaze

½ cup balsamic vinegar

1 tablespoon brown sugar

In a small saucepan, simmer the balsamic vinegar and brown sugar over medium heat until it reduces and thickens, about 5 minutes, and let cool.

Chocolate and Peanut Butter Truffles

1 package Nutter Butter cookies

1 (8 ounce) package cream cheese, softened

1 bag milk chocolate chips

1 tablespoon vegetable or Canola oil

Crush Nutter Butters in food processor. Cut softened cream cheese into chunks and add to food processor. Pulse until combined into a dough. Roll into small balls (about 1 inch). Freeze for 10 minutes on a cookie sheet. Melt chocolate chips in the microwave with 1 tablespoon oil. Stir until smooth and all chocolate is melted. Using a toothpick or spoon, dip the Nutter Butter balls into the chocolate, letting the excess chocolate drip off. Melt more chocolate, as needed. Set the truffles on waxed paper to cool.

And from Kristen's Kitchen...

Huckleberry Delight

2 cups graham cracker crumbs

1½ cups sugar, plus 3 tablespoons

8 tablespoons (1 stick) butter, melted

1 (8 ounce) package cream cheese, softened

1 (12 ounce) container whipped topping

3 cups huckleberries

¼ cup cornstarch

In a large bowl, combine the graham cracker crumbs, 3 tablespoons sugar and the butter together. Spread evenly in the bottom of a 9 x 13-inch baking dish. In a separate bowl, using a hand mixer, combine the softened cream cheese and ½ cup sugar until blended. Fold in the whipped topping and spread on top of the graham cracker crust. In a medium saucepan over low heat, combine the huckleberries, remaining 1 cup sugar and cornstarch, stirring constantly until sugar is dissolved and sauce has thickened. Let cool for 10 minutes, then pour over whipped topping layer. Cover with plastic wrap and refrigerate for at least 1 hour before serving.

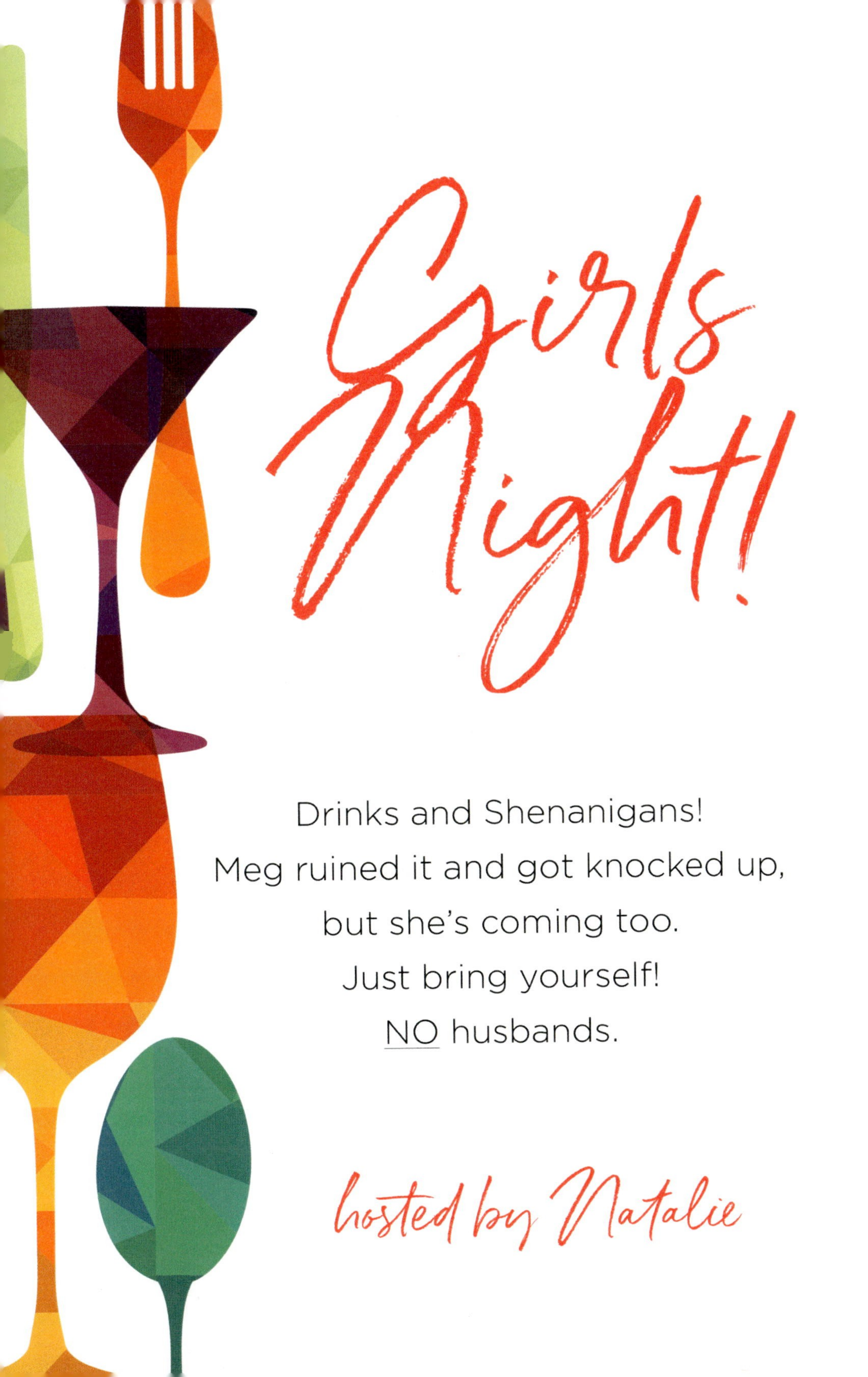
Girls Night!
Drinks and Shenanigans!
Meg ruined it and got knocked up,
but she's coming too.
Just bring yourself!
NO husbands.
hosted by Natalie

Luke & Natalie

Luke

"They're gone." I find my bride of six years in our closet, wearing only a matching set of light pink underwear and the pearls I gave her long ago, staring at her clothes as if she doesn't have anything to wear.

Trust me, she has plenty.

And I'll buy more for her, all she has to do is say the word.

She turns her smiling green eyes to me, a grin tickling her pink lips.

"Are you saying we're alone?"

"As alone as we've been in weeks," I confirm and pull her into my arms, holding her close. "I love our children, and I'd do it all over again any day of the week, but I do miss my alone time with you."

She sighs as I kiss her temple. "I know. Time alone is scarce these days. I just don't want to hire a nanny. I don't think we need one yet. Maybe when they get older and have to be shuttled around to this and that I'll want an extra set of hands, but I like it being just us for now."

"I don't disagree," I reply. "You're an amazing mother, Nat. No one is saying differently."

"I know." She smiles up at me. "Did you thank your parents profusely for taking them all?"

"Of course." She tries to turn back to her wardrobe options, but I hold her firm.

"Luke, I have to get ready. The girls will be here soon."

"How soon?"

"In less than an hour."

I feel the smile grow over my lips and Nat's eyes narrow on me. "We don't have time for this."

"Of course we do, baby." I nibble the side of her mouth, my fingertips barely grazing down her ribs to her hips. "We have plenty of time. You're already undressed."

She snorts as I lift her in my arms and carry her to the bed.

"Have I mentioned that I love your taste in undergarments?" I ask as I peel her panties down her legs.

"Only about four thousand times in the past six years."

"That's all?" I frown and press a wet kiss to her inner thigh, making her sigh in pleasure. She's added tattoos here over the years, the names of our children intertwined in a delicate design. I nibble my way to the apex of her legs and grin when her flesh erupts in goose bumps. "I love your underwear. I love it even more when it's wadded up on my floor."

She giggles and plunges her fingers in my hair, holding on as I drag my nose along the crease of her leg and over her shaved pussy, where she has ink etched on her mound.

I fucking love to trace her tattoos.

I kiss my way up to her belly and feel her tense. I know she's self conscious of the changes that four children brings to a woman's body.

"You're tensing."

She sighs. "The lights are on."

"Fuck yes, they are," I reply, kissing over the tattoo on her ribs. "I love looking at you, baby."

"I know, just consider it a woman thing."

"Your body has changed over the past six years, that's true," I murmur before licking the underside of the swell of her breast, making her sigh. "It's fascinating and beautiful."

"I wish I could get the stretch marks to go away."

"They're a road map," I reply simply. "A beautiful reminder of what your body went through to give us four healthy babies. I don't mind them in the least."

"You're sweet," she murmurs, then arches her back when I tug a taut nipple between my teeth. "And biased."

"I'm so fucking taken with you," I reply and let my hands glide over her skin, soaking in every delectable inch of her. "Everything about you, Nat. Your skin, your voice, the way you laugh. The way you sound when I do this."

I push two fingers inside her and make a come here motion, sending her body into a tailspin. She moans and grips the sheets in her fists, writhing on the bed. I plant my thumb over her clit and bite her neck, and that's all it takes to make her break apart into a thousand pieces, panting and biting her lip.

"That was one," I whisper into her ear.

"I really don't have time for more," she gasps, but I smile against her skin.

"Too bad. There's more."

Her hands are taking a journey over my body, up and down my back, over my ass, and up my sides. My cock is throbbing against my pants.

I need her.

I never stop needing her.

I reach between us and unfasten my fly, releasing my dick, and without hesitation, I slide inside her.

I slide home.

"Jesus," she moans, her hips already pulsing with the need to move, and I'm too fucking impatient to disappoint her.

"You're all I fucking think about," I growl as I lean on my elbows, cradling her head in my hands, and fucking her until we're both almost blind with it. "I never get enough of you."

"Jesus, Luke," she cries out and hitches her legs up around my hips, opening herself wider so I can push deeper, making me cross-eyed in sensation.

"That's right, baby," I whisper next to her ear. "I want you to come around me."

I reach between us to press on her clit once again, and I feel her begin to quiver as her orgasm moves through her. Her pussy is tight around me, milking me for all she's worth, and I know that I'm about to go over the edge with her.

We're panting, trying to catch our breath and return to earth. I'm still over her, but I've lifted onto my elbows again so I'm not crushing her.

"Know what else I love?" I ask her as I press a kiss on her swollen lips.

"Mm?"

"I love that you wear my pearls," I whisper. "Even when you're just staying in for a night with the girls."

"I love these pearls," she says with a soft smile. "I wear them with a lot of things."

"I know." I nuzzle her nose with mine, then roll away so we can start to get dressed again. "The kids are with my parents until tomorrow. I'm not staying away all night."

"Of course not," she says with a laugh as she pulls on her panties and adjusts her bra. "We can do some of this again later. In fact, I'll be pretty buzzed when you get home, so we can have drunk sex."

"You do enjoy the drunk sex," I reply and push her dark hair over her shoulder.

"And I've been pregnant for about twelve years, so we haven't had much of it lately."

"That might be an exaggeration." I wink at her and follow her back into the closet, where she chooses some skinny jeans and a simple black V-neck T-shirt.

With her pearls.

And somehow, on my Natalie, it works perfectly.

"Jules will be here soon," she says as she hurries to smooth her hair and brushes some gloss over her lips. "In fact, everyone will be here soon. But I think it's all ready."

"You'll have fun. You always do."

I follow her down to the kitchen, which is open to the living space. She's set the food up on the dining room table, and has a space prepared on the buffet for drinks.

"That's a lot of liquor."

She cocks an eyebrow. "Have you met us?"

"I'm glad you're staying home."

"We never drive when we have girls night," she reminds me. The doorbell rings, and I open the door to find Jules on the other side. She scowls when she sees me.

"No husbands tonight," she says. "It said so on Nat's invitation."

"I'm leaving," I assure her, closing the door behind her as she hurries in with a bag full of goodies.

"Everyone's on their way," Jules says with a smile. "And I do mean everyone. No one is sick, or has a sick kid, or is out of town."

"Awesome," Nat says with a happy shimmy. "We haven't had everyone together in a long time."

"And Anastasia hasn't been to a girls night since moving back to Seattle, so this will be a treat for her," Jules adds, referring to her cousin, who moved home earlier this year.

"I'm so glad I bought extra liquor. And food," Nat says.

She's in hostess mode now, and I know it's time for me to go. I'm going to spend the evening with some of the Montgomery brothers for poker night at Steven's house.

We haven't done that in a while either, and I've been looking forward to it.

"I'd better go, baby," I say as I pull Nat in for a kiss. "I'll see you later."

"Have fun," she says and stands on tip-toe to press her lips to mine. "I'll let you know if I need anything."

"Good."

"Ugh," Jules says, rolling her eyes. "Seriously, get a room. Or, better yet, you go."

She shoos her hand at me, making me laugh. Jules has always hated our public displays of affection.

I don't give a fuck.

Natalie

"It's never changed," Jules says after Luke leaves and I hear his car pull away from the house.

"What hasn't?" I ask.

"The kissing. The groping. It's as if you're still dating."

I smirk and pull the ingredients out for the charcuterie board. "We're in love, Jules. And don't give me that shit because I see the way you and Nate are."

"I know," she says with a sigh. "I'm happy for you. And me. And all of us."

"Me too. Now, help me set this out."

"You've transformed your whole table into a charcuterie board," she says with a laugh. "This is awesome."

"It's a lot of people," I reply. "We've grown."

"I know, and it's fun. But it's more difficult now to get us all together."

"So we're going to enjoy it tonight," I remind her.

Just as we're finishing up with displaying the food, Nic and Alecia arrive, followed by Meredith and Jax.

"I know I'm not a girl," Jax says, carrying one of Nic's bakery boxes. "But I bat for your team, and I need a night out."

"You're always welcome," I assure him. "Nic, thanks for bringing these."

"No, thank you," she says with a smile. "You're all my guinea pigs tonight. It's a new flavor."

"What is it?" Jules asks, peeking inside.

"Strawberry lemonade," Nic says with a smile. "And I've been told it's divine."

"I can't wait," Meredith says. "But first, I need a drink."

"I have a peach sangria, huckleberry lemon drops and champagne with pomegranate."

"Yes, please," Mer says with a laugh. "I'll work my way through all of those tonight."

"I can't believe I have to stay sober," Meg says as she walks in with Sam.

"I can make you virgin cocktails," I offer and giggle when Meg's smile turns naughty.

"It's been a minute since I was a virgin, but I'll take you up on it."

"No sex talk tonight," Jax says, pointing at all of us.

"Who's talking about sex without us?" Brynna asks as she and Stacy arrive, followed shortly by Amelia and Anastasia.

"Haven't you met us?" Alecia asks. "We drink and we talk about sex. That's what we do. You can't change the rules."

Jax reaches for the sangria. "I'll be working my way through all of these, too."

"Okay, now that we're all here," I begin, while we're all still sober. "I have a ton of food on the charcuterie board. And if we run out of anything, there's more in the fridge. Just let me know and I'll fill it back up.

"Also, there's a wet bar set up over there. I have a huge batch of peach sangria made, and have the fixings for huckleberry lemon drops and cham-poms."

"What's a cham-pom?" Sam asks.

"Champagne with pomegranate juice," Jules says with a wink. "And be careful because you'll get shitfaced on those things."

"I'll have two," Sam says with a laugh.

"Have I mentioned that I'm not happy about being sober?" Meg asks.

"You get to have a baby," I remind her and her face goes all gooey, making me laugh. "Just think about that. Here, I'll make you a huckleberry lemonade."

"That sounds really good," Meg replies with a smile and follows me over to the wet bar as most of the others make a beeline for the food. "Thanks for doing all of this."

"It's my pleasure," I say with a smile, mixing the lemonade and huckleberry syrup in a shaker with ice, then giving it a good shake before pouring it into a pretty glass. "Here you go."

She takes a sip and looks at me in surprise. "Wow. This is really good."

"Told you."

I spend the next twenty minutes mixing cocktails and making sure everyone has what they need before I make my own drink and load a plate with food.

"Nat, you have to see this," Stacy calls out, holding a photo in her hand.

"What is it?"

"Our baby," Nic says with a smile as Stacy passes the ultrasound photo to me. "She's going to be born in three months."

"Oh, Nic," I murmur, taking in the little nose and little fingers. "She's perfect."

"Do you get to be there when she's born?" Brynna asks.

"Yes, the first mom and I have been in communication, and she said that I can be there. She might not be confortable with Matt being there, but we'll see."

"You're calling her the first mom?" Jax asks. "That's interesting."

"It's accurate," Nic says with a shrug. "She's the baby's first mom, and I'm her forever mom." She smiles and bites her lip. "I'm really nervous."

"All moms are," I reply, holding my hand up in cheers. "Are you doing anything fun before she arrives?"

"Matt just told me that we're going to Italy next month," she says with a grin. "It's our last vacation away as a couple before we become a family, and I'm so excited."

"That's awesome," Jules says. "I know I've said it several times, but I'm going to say it again. I'm so happy for you both. I know how badly you've wanted this."

"Thanks," Nic replies with a grin. "I'm still pinching myself."

"Wait, shouldn't Nic be drinking a virgin drink with me?" Meg asks. "I mean, she's expecting, after all."

"You'll have to pry this liquor out of my cold, dead hands," Nic says with a laugh. "This is one of the perks of our situation."

"Kill joy," Meg mutters.

For the next hour we drink and eat and laugh, progressively getting more inebriated, until finally, everything is funny.

"I don't even know how to say charcoal board," Sam says with a frown. "But it sure is delicious."

"Charcuterie board," Jules corrects her. "Here, it's easy. Repeat after me. Char."

"Char," everyone in the room repeats, making us all dissolve into giggles.

"Cooter," Jules says. Brynna snorts sangria through her nose, making us all laugh even harder.

"Cooter," we all repeat once we catch our breath, still snickering like teenage boys.

"Ee," Jules says.

"Ee."

"Char-cooter-ee."

We repeat it about six times, giggling, until Sam finally says, "Yay! I can say it!"

"I've never been so happy to say cooter in my life," Jax says with a wink.

"Having a gay friend is so fun," Stacy says. "Let's talk about orgasms again."

"Again?" Jax asks. "Haven't we already covered this? Like fourteen thousand times?"

"We were drunk, Jax," Sam reminds him. "We forget."

"Meg should write it down," Amelia suggests. "Since she's sober."

"Way to rub salt in the wound," Meg replies with a scowl. "I'm not writing shit down."

"She's grouchy," Anastasia says with a laugh. "And if I'd known that girls nights were this much fun, I would have come way more often."

"I had orgasms today," I volunteer proudly. "Luke took the kids to his mom's and when he got home, bam. Orgasms."

"You always get them," Alecia says with a sigh. "But then again, I think we all do."

"We're lucky bitches," Jules says. "I've been feeling bad lately, though."

"Why?" we all ask in unison.

"So, Nate is awesome about going downtown, if you know what I mean."

We all nod, sipping and chewing.

"And I don't think I… reciprocate enough."

"I get it," Brynna says with a nod. "Sometimes I don't think I have a great technique."

We all turn to Jax, who looks around in surprise. "What? Why are you all looking at me?"

"Let's talk about blow jobs," Stacy says, batting her eyelashes. "Like, technique."

"I'm not drunk enough for this."

"Yes, you are," Alecia says with a laugh. "Come on, share some secrets."

"I don't want to lose my man card."

"You're sharing secrets that benefit men," I point out logically. "Obviously you can't lose your man card for that."

"I'll start," Nic says, clearing her throat. "I read a book where the woman went down on him, and when he's way in the back of her throat, she swallows, and that's supposed to massage the dick and be really great for him."

"I can see that," Jax says with a nod.

"But how?" Amelia demands. "I mean, doesn't she have a gag reflex? I don't mean to brag, but Wyatt isn't a small man."

"Same," several of us agree loudly.

"So," Amelia continues, "how in the world am I supposed to not only shove it to the back of my throat, but then also swallow around it and not throw up?"

"These are excellent questions," Brynna says, turning to Jax. "What do you think?"

"I think I should go home," he says, his cheeks turning red.

"No," Mer says, holding him in place, then pinching his mouth until he has duck lips. "Tell us the blow job secrets."

"Just suck it," he finally says. "Seriously, suck it, lick it, kiss it, stroke it. In any order. Any attention given to the dick is appreciated and will make him happy."

"But there has to be more to it than that," Sam says, disappointment written all over her face.

"Not really," Jax says with a shrug. "Guys are pretty simple."

"So you're saying that I should just give him the blow job, even if I don't think I'm all that good at it," Brynna says.

"Well, yeah. He comes when you do it, doesn't he?" Jax asks.

"Of course he does," Brynna replies.

"Well, there you go. He enjoys it. He wouldn't come if he didn't."

"Good point," Jules says, raising her glass. She reaches for her phone. "I'd better text Nate and let him know that I've learned all the blow job secrets."

"His is different," I remind her. "He's pierced."

"I don't know anything about that," Jax replies, holding his hands up in surrender. "I've never done that before."

"He still has a regular dick," Jules points out. "It's amazing, but it's a normal dick."

"But don't you have to be careful of the metal?" I ask, confused. "I'd be afraid that I was going to pull on it and hurt him or something."

"No," she replies, thinking about it. "He's never said that I've hurt him before. Shit, now I have to think about this. I'll text him."

She starts to type away on her phone.

"Nat, how do you spell dick?"

"Why does she always forget how to spell when she's drunk?" Meg asks with a laugh.

"Don't judge me, Judgy McJudgerson," Jules says with a scowl, staring at her phone. "How do you spell apa?"

"Jesus," Jax mutters, pulling his hand down his face. "I love you girls. You're a riot to hang out with."

"Damn right we are," I reply with a wink and glance over Jules's shoulder to see what she's typing.

"Who's Nick, and why are you texting him about sucking on his dick?"

"I'm texting Nate," Jules says.

"No, it says Nick at the top." I point to it, and she snorts.

"Fuck, good catch. Nate would have been really pissed if I'd sent that message to the business contact in New York."

"Oh, God," I mutter. "You should be banned from your phone when you're drunk."

"It's good now. See?"

She holds the screen up to me, and I see Nancy at the top of the screen.

"That's not Nate," I reply, covering my mouth to laugh behind my hand. "Oh, God, this is funny."

"Shit," Jules mutters, and holds it up again. "Now?"

"Now," Meg confirms. "But it says slit your dick rather than suck your dick."

"So?"

"Huge difference," Jax says with a laugh. "Enormous difference."

"Fucking autocorrect," Jules mutters as she corrects the mistake, concentrating harder than I've ever seen her before. "There. Whew, that was hard."

"Ask him for a dick pic," Sam says. "I want to see an apa."

"No way," I burst out with giggles. "No one wants to see that."

"I'm curious," Anastasia admits. "But he's her husband so, no. Not smart."

"We could Google it," Amelia suggests. "Then it's just a random dude's pierced..." she flails her hands about. "thing."

"Thing?" Meg repeats. "It's a cock."

"Exactly."

"Okay, I'll Google it," I offer, pulling my phone out of my pocket. When the images come up, I scowl. "Holy fuck, that has to hurt."

"I want to see!"

I pass my phone around the room. When it reaches Sam, she cocks her head to the side, examining it the way a scientist examines something in a petrie dish.

"Huh," she says. "It's not what I expected."

"It's not the Prince Albert," Jules says, shaking her head. "It's different."

"Yeah, I see that now," Sam says, pinching her fingers in and out to zoom in. "How long has he had it?"

"Years. More than ten."

"Wow."

"I'm going to text him and tell him you're all impressed by his cock."

"No," I say, pulling her phone out of her hand. "You'll misspell everything, and it's best if he doesn't know that we Googled it. Some things have to stay in the cone of silence."

"Fine," she says with a sigh. "Cone of silence on this one."

"Speaking of the cone of silence," Stacy says with a naughty smile. "I have to tell you something."

"If it's about sex with my brother, I'm not sure I want to know," Jules says, wrinkling her nose, but I wave her off and lean in.

"Tell us everything," I say.

"Well, you know Isaac and I have been married for over a decade, and sometimes you just have to spice things up, you know?"

"Carry on," Anastasia says. We're all fascinated to hear what she's going to say next.

Stacy takes a sip of her cham-pom. "Well, I've started dressing up in costumes."

"Like, a school girl?" I ask.

"That's one," she confirms. "I also have a naughty nurse, a belly dancer, a sea wench."

"A sea wench!" Sam exclaims, giggling. "Oh, that's awesome."

"It's fun," Stacy insists, laughing with us. "And I know it may sound silly, but it really does bring something fun and new to our sex life. He especially enjoys the belly dancer."

"I'm sure he does," I reply, giggling. "I'm going to have to try it. I bet Luke would be into it, having been an actor and all."

"Oh my God, you're totally right," Amelia says with a laugh. "Maybe I should try it. I have all the makeup in the world and I'm sure I have some outfits that would do the trick."

"All of our men are going to be stunned this week by our sea wenches and naughty nurses," I say, then turn to Jax. "What do you think you'll dress up as?"

"A sexy as fuck man," he says smugly. "That's all my man needs."

"Touché," Meg says, raising her empty glass.

"This is so fun, you guys," Jules says. "We need to do it more often."

"We always say that," Brynna says with a sigh. "But we're all so busy with kids and crazy lives, it just rarely happens anymore."

"We have to make it a priority," Stacy insists. "These nights fill my cup and make me happy. You're my tribe. I want to see you more often."

"Stop making the pregnant girl cry," Meg says, sniffling.

"I agree," I announce, holding my glass up. "More nights with our tribe."

"It's a deal."

Cocktails & Shenanigans

Huckleberry Lemon Drop

Sparkling Peach Sangria

Charcuterie Board

Cheese Crackers

Candied Pecans

Black-eyed Pea Hummus

Fig Jam

Pickled Banana Peppers

Strawberry Lemonade Cupcakes

Note from Kristen…

Pomegranate Champagne Cocktail

lemon juice (to rim the glass)

sugar (to rim the glass)

3 ounces lemon vodka

2 ounces lemon juice

2 teaspoons huckleberry syrup

1 lemon wedge

2 huckleberries

Rub lemon juice around rim of martini glass. Dip rim in sugar. Fill cocktail shaker with ice, vodka, lemon juice and huckleberry syrup. Shake to combine and pour into martini glass. Skewer a toothpick with lemon wedge and 2 huckleberries for a garnish.

Sparkling Peach Sangria

1 (1.5 liter) pink Moscato

1 cup peach schnapps

1 bag frozen peaches

1 (1 liter) Sprite

Mint leaves for garnish

Mix together Moscato, peach schnapps and peaches in a large pitcher. Refrigerate for one hour. Add Sprite and garnish with a sprig of mint before serving.

Charcuterie Board

I like to use 7 items but who's counting...Pretend that you are painting a blank canvas, only instead of paint you are using food. Your masterpiece will be a show stopper every time. Here are a few of my favorites that I like to pair with prosciutto, Brie, thin breadsticks, blue cheese stuffed olives and more.

Cheese Crackers

8 ounces extra sharp cheddar cheese

8 tablespoons (1 stick) cold salted butter

1½ cups bread flour

1 teaspoon salt

Preheat oven to 350 degrees. Grate cheese and butter, then blend for one minute in a stand-up mixer. Add the flour and salt and blend for an additional minute. Remove from mixer and knead for one minute, forming into a 1-inch disk. Place dough between two sheets of wax paper and roll out to ¼-inch thickness. Using a cookie cutter or a pizza cutter, cut out all crackers (making them no larger than 2 inches in diameter) and place on a greased cookie sheet. Bake in the oven for 12 minutes.

Candied Pecans

1 egg white

1 tablespoon water

1 pound pecans

½ cup brown sugar

1 teaspoon ground cinnamon

1 teaspoon ground nutmeg

1 teaspoon vanilla extract

Preheat oven to 250 degrees. Mix together the egg white and water until foamy with a hand mixer. Stir in remaining ingredients until pecans are coated and spread onto greased cookie sheet. Bake for 1 hour, stirring halfway through.

Black-eyed Pea Hummus

2 (15.5 ounce) cans black-eyed peas, rinsed and drained

2 tablespoons minced garlic

¼ cup olive oil

2 tablespoons tahini

2 tablespoons lemon juice

1 teaspoon paprika

1 teaspoon salt

1 teaspoon pepper

Place all ingredients in a food processor and process until smooth. Refrigerate for at least an hour before serving.

Fig Jam

4 cups figs

5 cups sugar

½ cup water

1 packet liquid pectin

6 jelly jars with lids

Puree the figs in a food processor or blender and place in a medium saucepan with the sugar and water. Bring to a boil over medium heat stirring constantly. After the mixture has been boiling for 1 minute, add the pectin and continue to stir for 4 minutes. Turn off the heat and allow to thicken for an additional 4 minutes. Ladle the mixture into the jelly jars leaving ½-inch headspace. Apply caps and let jam stand in refrigerator until set, about 12 hours, or transfer to a pressure cooker to seal for a longer shelf life. If you are not using a pressure cooker to seal the jars, the jam must stay refrigerated. Refrigerated jams are good for about 3 months and sealed jars have a shelf life of about 18 months to two years.

Pickled Banana Peppers

2 cups white vinegar

2/3 cup sugar

1 pound banana peppers, sliced into rings

6 (8 ounce) jelly jars

In a medium saucepan over low heat, bring the vinegar and sugar to a boil. Simmer for 3-5 minutes until the sugar has dissolved. Add the banana peppers to jelly jars and pour pickling mixture over them, leaving ½-inch headspace. Cover and refrigerate for at least a week before serving.

1 package yellow cake mix

½ cup oil

2 eggs

1 (3 ounce) package lemon Jell-O

1 cup orange juice

1 stick butter

1 (8 ounce) package cream cheese

½ cup diced strawberries

3 cups powdered sugar

Preheat oven to 350 degrees. In a large bowl, mix together the cake mix, oil, eggs, Jell-O and orange juice using a hand mixer. Pour the batter into 12 lined cupcake tins. Bake for 20 minutes or until a wooden stick comes out clean. While the cupcakes are baking, mix together the butter and cream cheese until fluffy. Add in the powdered sugar and mix until blended together. Stir in the strawberries. Remove the cupcakes from the oven and allow to cool completely. Top each cupcake with the icing using a piping bag or knife.

A NOTE FROM KRISTEN:

Hi friends! I wanted to include the pomegranate champagne cocktail in this book, or the cham-pom, because it's delicious, and it's absolutely true. You will get shit-faced quickly! It's seriously the perfect bubbly drink to have with your best girlfriends. Give it a try!

Pomegranate Champagne Cocktail

1 ounce pomegranate juice

3 ounces champagne

Sprigs of rosemary

Pomegranate seeds

In a champagne flute, add the pomegranate juice, then top with champagne. Garnish with a sprig of rosemary and 2-3 pomegranate seeds.

Index

APPETIZERS & SIDES

PASTRIES & SALADS

MAIN DISHES

DESSERTS

DRINKS

Other Books by Kristen Proby

The Big Sky Series:

Charming Hannah

Kissing Jenna

Waiting for Willa – Coming soon!

Kristen Proby's Crossover Collection

A Big Sky Novel: Soaring With Fallon

Wicked Force: A Wicked Horse Vegas/Big Sky Novella by Sawyer Bennett

All Stars Fall: A Seaside Pictures/Big Sky Novella by Rachel Van Dyken

Hold On: A Play On/Big Sky Novella by Samantha Young

Worth Fighting For: A Warrior Fight Club/Big Sky Novella by Laura Kaye

Crazy Imperfect Love: A Dirty Dicks/Big Sky Novella by K.L. Grayson

Nothing Without You: A Forever Yours/Big Sky Novella by Monica Murphy

The Fusion Series:

Listen To Me

Close To You

Blush For Me

The Beauty of Us

Savor You

The Boudreaux Series:

Easy Love

Easy Charm

Easy Melody

Easy Kisses

Easy Magic

Easy Fortune

Easy Nights

The With Me In Seattle Series:

Come Away With Me

Under the Mistletoe With Me

Fight With Me

Play With Me

Rock With Me

Safe With Me

Tied With Me

Burn With Me

Breathe With Me

Forever With Me

Stay With Me

Indulge With Me

Love With Me

The Love Under the Big Sky Series:

Loving Cara

Seducing Lauren

Falling For Jillian

Saving Grace

From 1001 Dark Nights:

Easy With You

Easy For Keeps

No Reservations

Tempting

The Romancing Manhattan Series:

All the Way

Southern Bits & Bites

Southern Kid Bits & Mom Bites

Southern Bits & Bites: Our 150 Favorite Recipes

Writing with Lexi Blake

Master Bits & Mercenary Bites

Master Bits & Mercenary Bites~Girls Night

Writing with J. Kenner

Bar Bites: A Man of the Month Cookbook

Writing with Larissa Ione

Dining with Angels

Made in the USA
Middletown, DE
22 September 2018